Susi...

"At first, I thought I could protect you—hold back the truth. Fool that I was," he went on, *"I even promised myself that I would ask nothing of you—"*

When he was silent, Loralei prompted an answer. "What do you want of me, darling?"

"The truth, Lory."

"You mean about the man—the one who boarded in Cabo San Lucas? I can explain—"

But Jerrod interrupted the little half-truth she planned. "About him, yes. But there is more. We've both behaved foolishly—kept secrets from each other. I can't ask you to share my life—such as I have or will have—until I share what I am. What I really am..."

CHOICE BOOKS
The Best in Family Reading
P. O. Box 503
Goshen, IN 46526
"We Welcome Your Response"

JUNE MASTERS BACHER is a highly gifted author who shares her talents in *Guideposts* and many other magazines. Her delightful stories and poems have become a trademark, including her most recent books, *Love Is A Gentle Stranger*, *Love's Silent Song* and *Diary Of A Loving Heart*. Now she brings her art to Christian romance novels, combining her storytelling with mysterious twists in the lives of her characters.

Until There Was You

June Masters Bacher

HARVEST HOUSE PUBLISHERS
Eugene, Oregon 97402

Other Rhapsody Romance books:

UNTIL THERE WAS YOU

Copyright © 1984 by Harvest House Publishers
Eugene, Oregon 97402

ISBN 0-89081-419-8

Printed in the United States of America.

With love,
to all members of the wonderful
Masters-Owens family,
my own!

"I could not love thee, Dear, so much,
  Loved I not Honour more."

—RICHARD LOVELACE, 1659

Chapter One

"*W*here to, miss?"

Loralei looked dazedly at the sleepy night clerk. Of course, he would need to know her destination. Otherwise, how could he know the air fare?

It was hard to make her eyes focus. The tear ducts were dry, having shed every reserve into the pillow where she had buried her head since the doctor pronounced her death knell just hours ago. "A year, Miss Coleman—maybe two at most—unless—"

But, covering her ears, Loralei had fled without waiting to hear more. *Unless some miracle occurred. Unless modern medicine came up with a cure they had been working on. All the things I've heard before. That's what they told Mother. And Mother died...*

"Miss?" the man behind the desk prompted.

Loralei's eyes, dry in their sockets, tried to make out the words on the myriad of exaggerated posters that seemed to float the circumference of the airport office.

Beaches at sunset...sailboats...thatched palapas...
sidewalk cafes. But the words blurred and the pictures
merged crazily into one. She squeezed her eyelids together
and tried again. This time she made out: MAZATLAN!
LAND OF ROMANCE.

Loralei shrugged. What difference did it make where
she spent her last days?

"Mazatlan," she said through wooden lips.

Loralei felt the desk clerk's eyes on her as she fished
in her bag for the right change. Studying her and apprais-
ing. The way Paul did before he commented on the things
he appreciated about her. The swinging gait of her tall,
slender height...every rise and fall, each hesitation, in
her voice...the way she angled her head to listen...even
what her fiance called the "translucency of her nostrils
and shell-like delicacy of her ears, the flecks of green in
her brown eyes"...Paul saw every detail in a way that
disturbed her sometimes—as if he had a lot of practice.
What would he say now—after her letter of good-bye?
Look for someone else probably...

Holding the money in her hand, Loralei looked up
from her bag to stare at the desk clerk. It was all so
unreal. Maybe he had interrupted a book she had been
reading. Only it wasn't from a book at all. It was life.
Her life—the one that was about to be snuffed out completely...at 24...

Loralei paid the man, she remembered later.

Did she have luggage to check?

Makeup kit and carry-on bag she had packed hurriedly before leaving the Santa Monica apartment she
shared with another girl. She would manage...

Was she all right? Oh, quite, she assured the man, steadying herself against the counter—just in need of cof-

fee. Plane loaded at 6 A.M. If she needed help? No!

Four hours and two cups of black coffee later she was looking down on the palm-lined beach of Mazatlan, dotted with tourists and strolling entrepreneurs. As the other passengers craned their necks for a better view of the tropical city on the Pacific, Loralei could only ask herself, *What on this green earth am I doing here?*

It had been foolish to board the plane. An impetuous decision. Totally unlike her. But then, she remembered bitterly, she had never been terminally ill before. That would excuse her spending almost all her cash reserve on a one-way ticket into a foreign country in the eyes of others who, like herself, were watching the last grains of sand drain from their hourglass of allocated time. But this was a foreign land with foreign customs. Knowing her passport was in order made her feel more secure.

The plane taxied to a stop. She unbuckled her seat belt but remained seated as the overly-anxious passengers shoved ahead. Then she made her way down the aisle. Hot, humid air rolled up from the pavement to wrap around her, the kind that sent little heat-wave mirages dancing over the rippled sand that stretched beyond the runway.

It was hard to breathe after Santa Monica's autumn-soft sea breeze. The white suit was wilting and Loralei felt her stockings sticking to her legs. She longed to peel them off on the spot. Instead, she picked up her kit and small bag and walked purposefully in the direction the others moved. *Shopping Center,* the sign read, although what she saw looked more like Arabian tents which appeared and disappeared with the arrival and departure of tourists by land, sea, and air.

Each step was a test in endurance. It was a relief

to see the sign *La Copa de Leche* where a smiling, dusky-faced waiter was lowering an awning. Maybe it was intended to give privacy to lovers. But to Loralei it was a haven from the merciless noonday sun.

"Leche, senorita?" The waiter bowed as she dropped into his proffered chair.

Loralei struggled with her high-school Spanish. "Milk?" she asked, feeling sure the man could speak English.

Leaning a bit too near, he said softly, "Milk—from the heart of a coconut!"

"Milk will be fine," she said, drawing back from the waiter's too-familiar manner. His words and his manner were offensive.

The dark eyes narrowed and the white-toothed smile disappeared. With a shrug, he stalked through the door of the sidewalk cafe. *So this is what it's like to be alone here, so obviously alone.* Add to that the fact that she was penniless. It would be nice to be able to pray again—pray and believe that God would hear the way He used to. But the legs of her faith had grown limber with her mother's illness and eventual death, and then crumpled completely when, in spite of her fervent prayers, she herself had fallen victim...

The waiter appeared with her milk. Setting it before her with a flourish, he leaned down and tried again. "La Copa becomes a nightclub at sundown and we serve stronger stuff—"

Loralei felt a panic rise up within her, stemming from all that had happened to her during the last 24 hours. "Go away," she whispered. "Please just go—"

She had heard no footsteps on the sand behind her so the deep masculine voice at her elbow was startling.

"You heard the lady!" Then, still behind her, the voice addressed Loralei. "I'll take care of the bill. You stay put."

I'm not going anywhere! Loralei stifled a hysterical laugh. She must pull herself together, thank the stranger—

And suddenly the stranger was back. Loralei's first impression was the towering height of the man. When at last her eyes reached his face, she knew immediately that it went with the voice. Not handsome exactly. Better than that. Interesting profile with high cheekbones and angling jaw to give it strength. The masculine features contrasted sharply with the stubborn wave in the dark hair— one, she suspected, that defied any comb that tried to straighten its curve. But the eyes were what caught and held her gaze—gray, intelligent, but haunted. Like her own...

Realizing that she was staring, Loralei felt color stain her face. "I—I'm sorry."

The man's smile was slow and easy. Yet it, too, was sad. "No problem, I assure you. I was doing some staring myself. Correction, some *admiring*. May I sit down?"

"Oh, of course! I should have asked you, for certainly I owe you my gratitude."

"Not at all. But may I suggest that you drink up and we'll move on toward the main section of town?"

Obediently, Loralei finished the drink, listening intently as the man introduced himself as Jerrod Barker, up for promotion with World Wide Computers. Home office in Kansas City. Branch offices all over the world. Yes, he traveled with the company. But, no—he was not on a business trip connected with WWC—not exactly, that is.

She noticed then that the haunted look came back. But, before she could lead him to say more, Jerrod Barker offered her his hand and pulled her to a standing position. Then, taking her bags, he led the way the short distance to the shopping center. There, as if lost in the novel she was reading, she watched as he checked her bags at a locker and followed when he motioned toward one of the larger shops. There, an ocean of cool, damp air reached out to mercifully lift the long hair from her shoulders...honey-colored, Paul used to say, with sunlight reflecting in it to match the green lights in her eyes.

But she wasn't going to think about Paul Teasdale. He was a chapter of the near-ending book—a chapter which was closed. Only a few pages remained, the here and now.

"We'll steer clear of the watering holes," Jerrod said with a teasing note in his voice. "Just visit some of the shops—you *are* new?" When she nodded, he continued, "Then don't be shy about bargaining."

They purchased a papaya, washed and sliced it, and munched as much of the enormous fruit as they could hold. No lunch, they agreed. Loralei, mentally counting pennies, bargained with Jerrod's help and bought a bright peasant blouse and skirt of cool cotton and a pair of straw sandals. She kept them on because of their coolness and had the sales clerk put her white suit in the shopping bag. When she turned from the counter, Jerrod was paying for a beautiful shell necklace that picked up the turquoise design in the new outfit.

She shouldn't accept a gift from a stranger, especially when it cost more than the outfit itself. But she seemed powerless to object. Why *was* she going off with some stranger in a foreign land? *I guess the standard precautions just don't matter anymore.* And in her mind Loralei turned another page of the novel, suddenly more interested in how it would end since she was the central character.

Once outside the maze of stores and none-too-clean stalls, Loralei was surprised to see that the sun was slipping down in the western sky causing noon-short shadows of the beach hotels to lengthen and stretch across the cooling sands. A first hint of the trade winds stirred the dozing coconut palms and mingled the scent of the nameless flowers with the overpowering scent of the sea as the fishing boats docked and unloaded their catch.

"Did you bring a hat?" Jerrod asked as they walked along a narrow street.

"No. Actually I don't own one."

"The sun can be cruel here. Unless you're tough-skinned?"

Loralei caught her breath. "I don't know—" she began, then stopped when she caught his gray eyes studying her face.

"We're all vulnerable sometimes," Jerrod said quietly as if he understood they were talking about more than the texture of her skin. "So," his voice changed to a lighter tone, "we'll do something about that. But not a hat, I think. I like what the wind does to your hair. We'll get an umbrella instead."

And before she could object, he had leaned over a barrel at one of the stalls, picked up a straw-colored umbrella, and opened it. "This one matches your sandals and doesn't try to steal the show!"

"Jerrod, no—" But he was paying for it and suddenly they were strolling the quaint village, hand-in-hand beneath the small umbrella's shade. *Like lovers! At the beginning—no, closing—of a book...*

Jerrod must have felt it, too. "You know," he said suddenly, "this place is not as cosmopolitan as Acapulco and lacks the charm of Puerto Vallarta. But it's said that if a honeymoon fails in Mazatlan, the marriage didn't have a chance to begin with!"

"That could be," she murmured, not exactly sure what was expected of her. She wasn't sure of anything really. What she was doing here. What was going to happen to her. Or how much she cared. Feeling would come back. But for now the numbness was a balm.

Jerrod broke into her thoughts. "Do you feel like walking?"

"I feel like doing anything!" Too late, Loralei realized her voice was defensive. "I mean," she said in a softer tone, "the breeze is cooling now, so a walk would be nice."

"Then let's try this cobblestone hike. Steep but the view's worth it."

Panting and breathless, they held onto each other as they struggled upward past the slanting, open-door, lean-to houses where naked children, pigs, and cackling chickens wandered in and out. Once Loralei stumbled and would have fallen except for Jerrod's strong hands. "Careful," he said softly. And then she was sure his next words were, "I wouldn't want to lose you...."

Her heart still pounding from the steep climb, Loralei drew a deep breath and lowered her umbrella. Then her eyes caught sight of the little church, sunlit and beautiful, with the bronze cross atop the towering steeple seeming to brush the cloudless sky. There was an enchantment about it, a singing, airy quality that seemed to strum some secret chord inside her. And then from somewhere in the tall tower a bell chimed softly, rising in volume until the gray walls of the little church caught the sound and gave back its echo.

"It's like the little church I used to attend when I visited my grandparents in the Sacramento Valley," she said with a catch in her throat. *The one where God lives,* she used to think. *Well,* she thought with a twist of bitterness, *that was probably true. They tore that little church down years ago and He hasn't answered a prayer since!*

"—computerized tintinnabulation, I call it. Oh well, it was just a dream I had." Loralei jumped, realizing that Jerrod had been talking and she had missed most of what he said.

"Dreams are important, Jerrod. Hang onto yours," she said, hoping that it made sense. And it seemed to for his voice was more eager when he spoke again.

"Actually, there would be no bells involved—at least, not the massive iron objects most people envision when they hear bells. Just little clappers that give out tinkling noises. A computerized carillon. The system would create the sound of seven large cast bells bonging away in programmed patterns...am I boring you?"

"No!" she said, meaning it. "Tell me more. I'm fascinated."

"Yes," he said softly, "yes, I guess you are! You know, you have a way of angling your head to listen that is most flattering—"

Paul's words. Her golden-bodied fiance. Only Paul, called the "Golden Boy" by his trainer, always talked of *his* ambitions—his plans to win a gold medal in the Olympics. Not about computerized bells for churches, colleges, and city halls. Who would share the highs and lows of his dreams now? No! She was not going to think about that chapter. Just concentrate on the final one.

In spite of the warm sun, she shivered.

Jerrod, lost in thoughts of his own, didn't seem to notice. "Would you like to go inside?"

Without waiting for an answer, he pushed open the narrow, weathered door which was long since stripped free of its paint, and entered the dirt-floored vestibule to make his way past the crude pews toward the front of the little church.

How long, Loralei wondered, had it been since she was inside a place of worship? Her father's being a colonel in the Air Force and her mother's fragile health robbed her of the usual little-girl practice of going to Sunday school. She had met the Lord at church camp in the High Sierras one summer and had the joy of introducing Him to her mother. He had answered her every prayer in those adolescent days. Then, suddenly, it was as if He didn't hear her anymore. Just when she needed Him most, God had turned His omnipotent back. Let her bear the heart-break of her father's death in an undeclared war...the hopelessness of her mother's condition...the losing of her. Oh, there was some Supreme Being up there some-where. The world was no accident. But a loving God? No, all thoughts of a Someone who loved her personally died along with her parents. Like Paul said, it was best to think of the anonymous creator in the abstract. Our short span on the Planet Earth was the whole show any-way...

In spite of her convictions, Loralei felt a familiar stir of semi-reverence at her surroundings, crude though they were. Most of the windowpanes were broken and only rough boards replaced them. But through the cracks tropical vines had crept in to drape the walls. Something looked inviting about the narrow pews with their faded kneeling benches and, without intending to, she sat down. It was then Loralei realized that Jerrod had reached the front of the church and was leaning against the pulpit, his head buried in his arms. *Something's troubling him. I should have known.*

As if having no will of her own, Loralei rose then and walked to where he stood. With his head still resting in the cradle of his right arm, Jerrod reached out with his left hand and laid it on her arm. His touch was gentle, as if he needed her strength. *Only I have none to give,* she though in quiet desperation. *Unless...*yes, maybe it was possible to encourage another to draw from his own well of faith without having any for herself.

"Do you believe in God, Jerrod?"

Jerrod lifted his head, his gray eyes filled with pain. "I have to, Loralei, I *have* to. There is no other way out."

The haunted look in his gaze wrenched Loralei's heart. And yet, she felt a strange sort of comfort at having said the right thing...

Outside the world lay in burnt-orange shadows as the sun, having lost its fierceness, dropped languidly into the sea. This man would need to be getting back to wherever he belonged. And she—well, where *was* she going? But they couldn't stand here and stare at a sunset, could they?

Yes, they could.

Transfixed, they seemed to sense the oneness here between the endless expanse of sky and the ever-restless ocean. Between man and nature. Between the two of them, strangers atop a little hill in a tropical port. And yes, admittedly a Oneness—a gentle yielding of all things to God...

Loralei came back to reality when Jerrod glanced at his watch. "I'm sorry. I've detained you—but, oh, I've never seen such a beautiful sunset," she said in a voice still choked with emotion.

"I know, Loralei," he said softly. "I know. It's as if it might have been the last."

Did he suspect her secret? Loralei jumped, but a sidelong glance at Jerrod's face told her nothing. Except that he was concerned about the time. Of course...he would be going somewhere. How on earth had this strange day come about anyway?

Jerrod took her hand and they started down the cobblestone path that wound into town. "Jerrod..." "Loralei..." They spoke together. Something to laugh about really. Only they didn't laugh. Instead they suddenly were in each other's arms in a tender embrace, the trade winds lifting her hair, winding it about his face, their lips touching in the most sad-sweet kiss she had ever known.

How could she be so intimate with a total stranger? But he *wasn't* totally foreign. There was something so familiar about him. *And this was the most important moment of her short life,* Loralei thought.

There were tears in her eyes when Jerrod released her. With all her strength she tried to hold them there, but to no avail. The drops spilled over one at a time, and then in a flood of emotion she had held back too long.

"Oh, Loralei, little sweetheart, don't!" Jerrod's voice was so shaken with sadness he could scarcely speak. Oh, she had no right to burden him like this with her problems, her hopelessness...helplessness...fears. He was a stranger! Only he wasn't, of course. He was the man she had known and searched for all her life. Only he had come too late. Too late.

★   ★   ★

Here and there the streetlights twinkled on. Tanned-bodied surfers brought their surfboards ashore. Houses closed, some of them barred against the night, and restaurants opened after the afternoon's siesta. Jerrod glanced at his watch again, a little nervously this time. Then, with a slight shrug, he seemed to reach a decision.

"You must be starved. No lunch except for that papaya!"

And only black coffee as a substitute for breakfast. Yes, suddenly she was ravenously hungry—probably due to the bracing sea air. Her silence answered his question.

"Free meals at the bars, but that's out. Right?"

"Right."

"Mamucas probably has the most inclusive menu—frog legs—"

"Ugh!"

Jerrod laughed and she joined him. "You're giving all the right answers, young lady," he said with a warm squeeze of her hand. "El Shrimp Bucket attracts a lot of tourists, providing they know a cruise ship's in port, so we'll act like long-time residents. How would you like a basket of hot, fresh-fried prawns, a loaf of bread—and a melange of fresh fruit juices served in coconuts, straws included!"

"Fun!"

"Great, then we'll sit in the courtyard and watch the crowds. We can see the ocean from there—maybe take a stroll—if there's time."

The heavy moments of the afternoon were gone. Light-heartedly, they chatted away as they finished every morsel, testing this sauce and that.

There was a bad moment when two uniformed police-men stepped out of the giant hibiscus shrubs and stood surveying them in what appeared to be hostility. Loralei felt her face blanch. Had they come to question her presence here already? But how foolish! How could they know? Turning to Jerrod, she smiled with relief. But her smile died before it reached the corners of her mouth. His face was ashen in the fluorescence of the streetlight at the corner.

"Jerrod!" she said in alarm, forgetting the two Mexican officers.

"It's all right, officers. I'll take care of matters. I—"

But the men did not seem to be listening. "This yours, miss?" the heavier of the two bulky men asked. As he spoke, he leaned down to pick up her shopping bag into which she had tucked her wallet.

"Yes, and I have my passport—"

The man shrugged to his partner and spoke something inaudible in Spanish. Then, turning back to Loralei and Jerrod, he said in clipped English, "Better find a private nook elsewhere. Better keep an eye on your valuables, too. Easy place to get ripped off."

Relieved, Loralei was effusive in her words of appreciation. Later she recalled that Jerrod had not spoken again.

Somewhere there was a long blast of some giant horn followed by a tinkle of bells. It was just a part of the night to Loralei, but it must have had a meaning to Jerrod. For the third time, he glanced at the watch on his tanned wrist. Time had lost all meaning to Loralei. But a little advice of her mother's when she first began dating came back: "It should be the young lady who sets the pace and that includes drawing the evening to a close."

With a purposeful motion, she rose from the bench. "My! I really *must* be going," she murmured, hoping that her voice sounded convincing.

Jerrod made no protest. Picking up the remains of their park-bench feast, he said, "It is I who has extended the day. Selfish of me, but," dumping the trash into a barrel, "I'll see you to your hotel."

"Oh, no—no—please! That's impossible!"

"You heard what the officers said."

Loralei forced a smile. "There's a reason," she said, trying hard to fake a mystery by rolling her eyes skyward. "And I'm safer than safe. The two policia are still there and they'll take me—"

Sooner than you know, she should have added.

Jerrod looked unconvinced. But when there were three more short, insistent blasts of the horn, he lowered his head in silence. Then in a shaken voice he said, "I want you to know, Loralei, that this has been the happiest day of my life. I will treasure it forever. *But never try to see me again.*"

The finality of his tone broke her heart. And then Loralei realized how irrational such thinking was. For her there *was* no future. Maybe no next year, the doctor had said. Maybe no tomorrow if the authorities found out she was stranded here. Under normal conditions, she would have gone to the American Consulate...surely there was one here. But then, under normal conditions, she wouldn't be here. And most assuredly she wouldn't have spent the day with a man she had never seen before.

But she could feel no remorse at what others would cheapen by calling a "pickup"...just a deep sense of sadness that it was to be their last day together as well.

With a start, Loralei realized that Jerrod was studying her, his gray eyes—now silver in the light—filled with concern. "Something is troubling you, little Lory. Is there anything—*anything*—I can do that will ease the pain in these few minutes we have left?''

Numbly, she shook her head.

"I wish to God that things were different—for us both."

She nodded, still unable to speak.

Then without warning Loralei was back in his arms again, her wind-tossed hair wrapping around the strength of his shoulders in the same warm curve she had found before. She found her voice then to say, "Jerrod, we're not strangers—it seems we've met before—and stood like this. It's like we've spent our entire lives together—''

It was he who tore himself away. "Don't, Lory, don't! I have to leave you. Just sit there in that pool of light and let me look at you. That's a girl. Close your eyes. Don't watch me leave—and I, with the help of God, won't look back—''

His voice trailed into the night. And when at last she opened her eyes, the darkness had swallowed him up. And the two officers were walking slowly toward her.

It didn't matter. Nothing did. It was as if this golden day had never been. . . .

Chapter Two

*B*ehind Loralei there was a sudden clop-clop of horses' hooves on the rough streets. Turning away from the approaching policemen, she found herself face-to-face with a merry group of tourists who were being helped down by a smiling, uniformed driver of the horse-drawn carriage. "Th' arana she *was* funny, yes?"

"Oh, funny, funny, fun-*nee!*" a shrill feminine voice answered. "But if you've caused us to miss our ship—"

There was an excited buzz of voices as guests tipped hurriedly and scrambled toward the harbor. The last of the passengers was leaving, a beautiful girl about her own age. Loralei stared. She couldn't help it, because of the girl's dark vibrancy even in the semi-darkness and because of something else she was unable to put her finger on. How could the young woman be so wholesome and yet so provocatively female? Her dark sable hair swung long and straight to her shoulders, curling softly at the ends to break the severity. Her complexion had the clean look that comes from outdoor living and good care. It glowed golden with a light suntan, radiating a warmth that was familiar... or was it just a familiar feeling? The kind that comes from admiring another person almost to the point of envy? That had to be it... the girl was so *alive!*

Seeming to sense eyes on her, the girl turned with a quick fluid motion that began with her dark hair and rippled along the muscles of her rounded hips. Graceful as a doe, she sprang forward with a sudden motion that caught Loralei totally unprepared.

"Loralei! Lory Coleman! Class of '81—Miss Agatha's Girls' School. It *can't* be you!"

"Amy—oh, Amy!" Loralei's voice was no more than a whisper in the night air. But how could Amy Farrell, her former college roommate, who by her own admission was as wealthy as she was beautiful, be here?

Loralei felt a faint dizziness that threatened to turn into nausea. The shrimp, no doubt. And maybe they were causing hallucinations. Could she be imagining Amy?

And maybe, she thought with something akin to panic clutching at her heart, *I imagined Jerrod as well.* No, they were real—real like characters in a book.

But it was a very real pair of hands that pulled her to her feet, embraced her warmly, and began in her usual quick, breathless way, "Gotta hurry—I'm *always* the late one—who're you staying with? Come on, walk me to the ship."

And at the sudden blast of the horn that had alerted Jerrod's ears, Amy screamed, "Oh, for the love of Mike, we've got to run for it! Come *on!*"

Pulled by the hand as she was, Loralei had no recourse but to make her weak legs carry her forward. It was always like this, she remembered—being tugged along by her vivacious friend when Amy's parents came from New York to spend winter vacations in Santa Monica. It was the same way when Loralei, at her mother's insistence, attended the expensive private school in New York with Amy. It had taken all her father's insurance money that Loralei's mother could spare. But it was hard to fight against Mrs. Coleman, Mrs. Farrell, Amy—and her own temptation.

So she had allowed herself to be tugged along to do what was "so necessary for young ladies." Actually, the little course in commercial art that she took the following year was the more practical—even more interesting. It had landed her the job she held now. Not that it paid much. She ought to look around, be more ambitious, others told her, in much the same way that Amy had advised her about meeting new boys. But Loralei liked what she was doing.

Loralei remembered how Amy had rounded out, begun experimenting with lipstick, and eventually moved on to dancing and dating while she clung to the security of childhood. She needed the known, the familiar. Well, that too was gone now...even though she had met Paul whom Amy would approve of...

They were nearing the harbor. Amy had kept up her incessant chatter, flinging words over her shoulder as she ran. Most of her conversation was lost to Loralei, but she caught fragments. Amy was between romances. In need of adventure. Mother is in Europe—separated from Daddy, you know. Daddy's religion is his work— Mother's is the bright lights! Only Amy was bored, *bored*...so, the cruise.

Did she remember Roz Vandercroft? No, Roz came a year later. "Roz is sharing the suite with me—"

Amy's voice trailed away only when they reached the gangplank of the enormous white ship, its lights flooding the harbor and smokestacks steaming impatiently against a velvet sky.

Exhausted from the run, Loralei tried to pull back as Amy hurried up the gangplank.

"We're late, miss," she heard one of the men at the top telling Amy. "There's a storm at sea and—"

But Amy waved him away and, turning back to Loralei, she cupped her hands to make her voice carry above the noise of the ship's engines, *"Lory!"*

Panting and still fighting the dizziness, Loralei moved up the damp gangplank.

"Your pass, miss?"

"She's with me," Amy said airily as if that explained everything.

"Sorry, miss, no visitors. As I said, we're late and the storm—"

But Amy was tugging at Loralei's arm. Pulling her past the two white-uniformed men. "She'll only be a minute, I promise." With that, she turned toward the men with her irresistible smile, the one Loralei remembered so well because of its hint of mischief. That smile could melt a glacier.

This was no exception. The men nodded, called a word of caution which was lost to Amy, and they were aboard—*the way it happens in books,* Loralei thought, feeling an overwhelming sense of euphoria.

Inside the halls, she had entered a storybook setting of warmth, comfort, and luxury. She watched the laughing passengers moving past her to wave at a familiar face or to pause when elevators and stairways were filled to chat amiably with strangers. Forming and reforming groups so casually. Intermixing and mingling. Never seeming to make permanent attachments. Maybe that's the way it was with the idle rich. Far cry from the world she lived in where there wasn't enough money to purchase a ticket for returning home.

Up the red-carpeted stairs. Down the bronze-carpeted hall. And Amy was fumbling with the key to her stateroom.

"This is it!" she said when the door burst open.

"It—it's lovely," Loralei murmured, her mouth feeling dry, her senses dulled by all that had happened in one day.

"Could've had cheaper ones—smaller and with one porthole—even *none*—but I prefer the best."

Together, they explored the room with Loralei making what she hoped were the right comments. One part of her wanted to join in on the unexpected pleasure of this chance meeting. But the other part was straining to hear a possible warning that all visitors must go ashore immediately.

"I could show you around—the theatre, casino, dining room, lots to see—but, no, let's not waste time. Sit down and tell me all!"

Totally oblivious to time, Amy fell down across one of the sofa beds and motioned Loralei to the other.

Loralei's legs were too tired for her to resist. Just a moment, she promised herself, and no more. She had to get off that ship on time!

"Now! Let me look at you! You've changed. Oh, I see why I had to do a double take to recognize you—you've given up glasses for contacts?" Amy's tone was admiring.

Loralei, feeling uncomfortable as she always did when

attention was focused upon her, nodded. "It was you who suggested them."

"And rightly so. Why, you've blossomed. I know! You're in love."

"Well—yes—yes, I guess I am."

"Tell me all about him."

Which one? Loralei wondered with a heavy heart. *The one I left behind? The one I just met? The one I was supposed to marry or the man I want to spent the rest of my life with? The rest of my life...oh, Amy, do you know how short a time that can be?*

But her friend was filing an acrylic nail and did not look up to see the pain that crossed her face. Loralei was glad.

"Go on," Amy urged. "It's that Greek god, isn't it? The 'Golden Boy' you wrote me about—when was it, last Christmas?"

Loralei nodded. Might as well plunge ahead. Amy would tease the information out of her anyway. She wondered for the millioneth time why Amy had bothered with her in the first place—the stringy 14-year-old she had been that first winter of their acquaintance.

Probably they would never have met except that their mothers belonged to the same garden club for a short time and encouraged a friendship between her and the beautiful Amy who was everything she herself wanted to be. Self-assured. Comfortable around people of all ages—and absolutely captivating around the boys.

Even at 15, Amy's ears were pierced and she wore shining gold loops attracting an even larger audience of boys. Loralei felt that she was like the earrings. No will of her own. Going everywhere Amy went. Just dangling. Boys didn't look at her. And she didn't look at them. One had to acknowledge that they existed, of course. But one didn't have to expect them to love or be loved.

Even now the pain of the realization hurt...it had squeezed her heart dry. Until she met God. And now she had to put Him in the same perspective...

Did she imagine the sudden tilt of the ship? Probably a part of the dizziness she had come to accept. That was the symptom that had taken her to the doctor in the first place...

"Lor—*eee!* You're teasing me about this What's-his-name—Paul?"

"Oh, Paul—" Loralei came back to the present, "I guess the engagement's off. I prefer it that way for right now."

Amy, who changed romantic interests as often as she changed hairstyle, nodded.

"So you're trying your wings elsewhere! You know, I just never thought you had it in you. I wish I had known, but an exchange of Christmas cards doesn't give us much chance to exchange confidences."

Amy continued obliviously, "There's this special deal, you know—taking an extra person along on the cruise, would you believe *free?* Roz and I paid for double occupancy and the third would have been a bonus—"

The ship *did* tilt! Alarmed, Loralei rose clumsily to her feet. They could be casting off at any given moment. "I have to go this minute, Amy—"

Before her sentence was finished, the door burst open to admit Roz Vandercroft, a short, freckled redhead with round blue eyes.

Before there was time for an introduction, the girl gasped, "Don't tell me you're a guest! Oh, I hope you boarded at Mazatlan!"

"No—I didn't board at all—what I mean is, I *am* aboard—but—" And with a jumble of words, she tried to reach the doorknob.

Amy had pulled apart the porthole drapes. "For the love of Mike!" she screeched. "We're at sea!"

Chapter Three

*L*oralei awoke sometime during her first night at sea, aware of a gentle rocking as if she were lying in a hammock on a lazy afternoon. Vaguely, she wondered where she was. Then it didn't matter. She drifted back into a dreamless sleep of exhaustion.

Neither were her surroundings clear when partial awakening came the next morning. From behind closed eyelids she heard familiar voices, but she was too close to the netherworld of slumber for the speakers or their conversation to sound strange.

"Let Sleeping Beauty sleep. That was some day she had yesterday," Amy whispered and the two girls giggled.

"Any trouble making arrangements for a third occupant?" That was Roz.

"None. Fortunately Loralei had her wallet and I could furnish I.D. from the passport. Odd thing, her remembering that her one bag and makeup kit were in a locker—and that some strange man she met *yesterday* forgot to give her the key! Unlike the old Lory—but kind of good, you know? She used to be so withdrawn, living in her own little world—"

"But isn't she the one who set *you* straight at Miss Agatha's? I would have thought she was your model." Roz's voice was muffled as if she were shuffling around in the one closet the three of them must share.

In the bathroom Amy was splashing water. "Oh, she was, only she never knew. I was such a mixed-up kid. She's the one who got me going on the 'faith' thing, you know. But it's good to see that she's decided it's O.K. to have fun and feel that God approves."

Roz was still fumbling in the closet. "You can't possibly use all these clothes, Amy. I've no room! Why did you bring so many?"

"My style, I guess. But it paid off for once. Poor Lory's stuck without a rag and we're just the same size. So!" There was a triumphant note in her voice.

A few minutes later both girls tiptoed to the door. "Put the *Do Not Disturb* sign out, Roz," Amy whispered. "Lory'll miss the first seating at breakfast, but she can try for the second."

"Or snack on deck. It's another one of those beautiful mornings—ooops!"

Both girls drew back inside. "Guess who I just saw?" the voice was Amy's. "Our mystery man—and I just had to drop back to tell you something. I caught a glimpse of him yesterday at Mazatlan."

"You mean—" Roz's voice was incredulous, "you mean he went ashore after passing up Acapulco, Zehuatanejo, and Puerto Vallarta?"

"Right!" Amy was peeking into the hall again. Then she added, "*And* with a woman! At a church!"

The door closed soundlessly and Loralei lay heavy-lidded in her bunk. If she lay very still it would all come back. Something would make sense. There was a shrill ring of the telephone and Loralei found herself fumbling for the instrument among assorted bits of clothing, souvenirs, and unopened mail.

"Yes?" she managed.

"Miss Coleman?" How could anyone know her name? "This is your purser speaking. We have a response to your cablegram."

Cablegram? Oh yes...cablegram...the one Amy had helped her phrase to her roommate to say where she was and ask the other girl to tell Loralei's boss she was taking the week's vacation worked up from overtime.

Would Miss Coleman like the steward to deliver the cablegram?

Everything was paid for Amy had said. Except gratuities. And Loralei wasn't sure whether guests paid with each service or at the end of the cruise. *End of the cruise! Where on earth were they going anyway?*

There was a faint sigh at the other end of the line. "I'm sorry," Loralei murmured. "Would you mind just reading it aloud?" There surely would be no charge for that small service.

Loralei listened to the brief message the purser read with his crisp British accent. Stunned, she thanked him and replaced the phone on its cradle. Immediately she regretted not asking him to reread it. What could it mean? And how did the sender know?

"You're out of your mind. Stop. Must see you. Stop. Your place or mine?" And it was signed, the purser said, "Paul."

And then came the flooding realization of what she had

done. Invitations to the small wedding were to have been addressed and mailed this week according to the schedule Paul had worked out with his mother. Otherwise, the groom wouldn't be able to attend! Although Loralei had teased Paul about that, deep inside it had hurt a little that anything as important as their wedding had to be wedged between his training program and Olympic tryouts. No honeymoon either...

"Well," she said aloud, her heart twisting inside, "Paul was right about that—only—" biting her lip to hold back the tears, "there will be no wedding either—no life together. No *life!*"

When, moments later, her emotions were under control, Loralei realized it was easy to put the rest of the story together. Paul must have called her roommate. He was to have helped with the addressing and would have needed to find out when to come over. Her hours had been so long at the office, depending on how much of a hurry clients were in for the sketches she made for their advertising layouts. And that made Paul cross. One had to be organized, he said. Have a time for everything.

He was right about that, too. For all things a season. A time to be born and a time to die. Only Paul wasn't quoting Ecclesiastes. His bible was his training manual. But Jerrod—

Jerrod! Yesterday's memory washed over Loralei then, drowning her with its beauty. It had been a dream walk. And yet it was the greatest reality she had ever known. How could anything so fragile be so strong—so lasting? One day together. That's all they had been allowed. But it was the kind of day that turned stumbling blocks into stairs. Stairs that began on earth and led to heaven.

Weak-kneed, Loralei sank back onto the stool from

which she had risen. "No further questions, Lord," she murmured without realizing she was making it a prayer. "I know the answer. It's love—the kind that comes to a woman only once in a lifetime. And only then if she's very, very lucky."

Lucky? When death was closer than Jerrod? How could a God who created this universe be so cruel? How could He not care? Well, she mustn't care either. She owed herself these days which fate and Amy had arranged. She owed that to her friend. And something more. At the thought, Loralei frowned. Amy, she remembered, had told Roz that she was into what she called "this faith thing." And because of Loralei. It would be unfair, she reasoned, to destroy Amy's new-found faith just because her own had crumbled.

Loralei picked up yesterday's clothing and headed for the shower with a shrug. What was the harm of playing along?

In the shower, Loralei felt her spirits rise. The sting of the water relaxed her muscles, made her want to live out the day, purposeless as it might have sounded a moment or so before. As she toweled herself dry, she felt an urge to sing. Something deep inside was trying to surface. Something which accounted for this happiness. She reached for the toothbrush Amy had provided, claiming she always brought along six extras, and caught her eyes in the mirror. They were, as she suspected, giving off little green lights. What was the secret for such irrational feelings? There had to be a key—

Key! That was it. Jerrod had her key! Somehow he would find a way to return it to her. And they would be in touch again. Oh, blessed thought! It was such a tenuous link. But it would work. It *had* to! She would die if it didn't—at that thought Loralei had to laugh at herself. And the laugh felt good. Yesterday she would have been willing to say good-bye forever, knowing how brief a time would remain for them, but today was different. She would take any crumb she could get. She knew how precious each moment was...

With a light step, she ran up the first flight of stairs leading toward the sun deck, according to the directory in the lobby. On the landing she paused when the ship gave a great heave and pitched forward before righting itself. Clawing at air, Loralei would have fallen had some faceless stranger behind her not reached out a hand to steady her.

"Hang onto the rail," he advised. "Rough seas this morning, but the clouds make a beautiful sunrise."

On deck the air was clean and pure. Loralei hurried past the long table packed with such a variety of food it must have come from kitchens all over the world. She felt hungry, but never in a million years would there be another such sunrise. She hurried to the rail and gazed in awe at the crimson clouds, their insides lined with purest gold, that piled up in the east as if to delay the sunrise. Uneasy as the tides that washed below them, the clouds moved to change shapes and color, sometimes deepening from crimson to purple and finally to a deep mahogany before dissolving to reform like cumulous cathedrals. Wasn't it the most beautiful sunrise in the world? Or was it because she saw it from a new perspective—as if she were counting her sunrises now? Strange how life had changed so quickly—making her see people, values, all the phenomena of nature as infinitely more precious than before.

Regretfully, Loralei turned from the darkening eastern

sky. Waiters would be taking the food away soon and she didn't want to miss her first meal ever aboard a ship. Tempted to linger and admire the artistic flair the cooks had added to every dish, she hurried along the table. Choosing was hard. Juice or fresh fruit? Oh, the fruit boat—the *big* one with lots of papaya, she thought tenderly. Cereal, fresh breads, waffles, ham, little sausages. And English muffins with some of the melon conserve, a boiled egg and lots of coffee!

Laughing at her own plate, Loralei stretched herself out on a chaise lounge, choosing to hold the tray on her lap to bask in the occasional splashes of golden sunlight that swept aside the curtain of clouds.

Never had the sun felt so warm, so life-giving. And never had food tasted like this. It was as if her taste buds, like her heart, had been sleeping, waiting to be awakened by the kiss of the beloved Prince Charming she had read and dreamed about until—finally realizing that such things happened only in books—she had folded the dream.

Stretching like a kitten, feeling fit and well-fed, she put on her dark glasses and lay lazily watching the crowds from her resting place.

Soon she must look for Amy, let her know she was all right. There would be a host of questions for them both. But for now she would watch the wealthy at play. If she could be this happy in her desperate set of circumstances, they must be ecstatic!

But they didn't look happy. They didn't look happy at all. Golden, oiled bodies, in abbreviated swimming suits drifted by her. Girls bored. Couples sharp with one another. Middle aged people seemed intent on faking a good time, each couple seeming to concentrate on how to impress or outdo the other couples. There were pouchy men who middles hung over their swimming shorts eyeing women half their age. And women with purple-veined legs wearing bikinis but staying away from the water to preserve their well-coiffed hair. The man next to her was complaining about his sunburn. His wife was fanning herself and saying the humidity here was worse than Florida's—so why had they come?

Desperate people. Miserable—

It was then that a beautiful fantasy occurred in her mind. Jerrod was here. The two of them stood by the rail of the ship and watched the gathering clouds until the breeze stiffened and blew her hair about his face. Holding it, he pulled her gently to him . . . and then they settled together in a sheltered spot where they sat holding onto each other as the sun reached its zenith and sank in another flame of glory like yesterday's—like *all* their sunsets would be.

The moon came up and rode high, then paled, and as the pink fingers of dawn touched their bodies, they trailed quietly hand-in-hand to their separate cabins. Disturbing nobody. And not wishing to be disturbed lest someone awaken them from their wordless dream walk of love.

So different from *these* people. So *alive!*

At first, Loralei was not sure the man was speaking to her when he said softly, "Miss?"

"Miss!" he said louder, and she opened her eyes out of curiosity, though reluctant to leave her dream.

The man's eyes, behind horn-rimmed glasses, were friendly enough, his manner pleasant. But something about his demeanor alerted her. For some unaccountable reason she knew he was a law enforcement officer even before he removed a card of identification from his vest pocket.

"Miss Coleman, I believe?"

Loralei sat upright. What could be wrong? Where was Amy?

"Nothing to be alarmed about, I assure you," the man said, introducing himself as Captain Max Avery of the Federal Bureau of Investigation. "But do these items belong to you?"

He held her carry-on bag and makeup kit in front of her. Stunned, Loralei could only nod foolishly.

"They led us to you," he explained, "and I'm afraid we must ask your help. Mexican officials opened the locker for us when you did not return the key—"

"There's nothing of importance in them. Feel free to examine them!" Loralei said hurriedly.

Captain Avery smiled. "Thank you, Miss Coleman. We have done that. But it concerns another matter. Do you happen to know a man by the name of Theron Stone?"

"No, sir," Loralei said slowly. "The name means nothing to me—nothing at all. But I am wondering why you think he has anything to do with me?"

The captain hesitated. "It could be just a coincidence," he said. He thanked her and was about to move away when he turned suddenly. "If he should contact you, you will call me?"

Accepting his card, Loralei nodded mutely.

What on earth was this all about? There must be some silly mistake, of course. Some kind of mistaken identity. Security must be tight with passengers from all over the world on a British ship with Italian chefs and French entertainers floating around in Mexican waters.

Hoping the questions were more or less routine, she settled back to collect herself before looking for Amy.

Closing her eyes against the glare of the glassed-in wall, Loralei may have dozed. Or maybe what happened next followed immediately. Exit one man. Enter another. She couldn't be sure of much these days. She only knew that it was natural. Right. The normal sequence of events when one is caught in a world of deja vu.

"Was the man annoying you, Lory?"

No need to open her eyes. She would remember forever the voice with deep bass-notes of a softly ringing bell. No need to check on the height. Even behind closed lids, she could feel that the shadow falling across her on the lounge was tall. Broad-shouldered. Lean but powerful.

"Oh, Jerrod—Jerrod! You're here—" was all she could manage. How, when, why did not matter. Just that they were together.

"Of course, I'm here," Jerrod whispered close to her face as if their meeting were prearranged. "I had to return the key."

In real life, it would have made no sense. But real life does not last. This dream world where one asked for no tomorrow was better.

Loralei was thankful for the darkness behind the sunglasses. The sight of the masculinity of the dear, wonderful face—the love that would be shining in his hauntingly beautiful eyes—would be more than she could bear. It was enough just to feel his warm fingertips slipping the key into her hand, trailing up her bare arm until they reached her face, then tracing every outline of her own face tenderly.

"Stay," she whispered, hoping they could live out her fantasy.

"I wish it were possible," Jerrod whispered, his breath warm against her ear. "Such a lovely ear—like a dainty shell. I'm glad you don't cover it up with earrings."

The light brush of his lips against her ear was a kiss of farewell. She knew that. Just as she had known it was preordained that he should go.

"Oh, Jerrod—we—we'll meet again? We—" Loralei longed to grasp at his clothing, to pull him down beside her, to plead.

But no! She would not so much as open her eyes. Jerrod might vanish.

Jerrod's laugh was low, deep, and frighteningly real. "Of *course* we'll meet. Until tonight, little Lory—I'll find you."

Jerrod's fingers slipped from her face. And he was gone.

It was fitting that he should go. Dreams must end. Why, then, did tears well up, overflow, and roll down her cheeks as she sat motionless where Jerrod had left her?

"Lory! Loralei Coleman!"

Amy's voice always reached her before her friend ever did.

Loralei wiped at her eyes and was ready to make some excuse to the breathless Amy who was too excited to notice the tears.

"I can't believe my eyes! You're a constant surprise—you are—one of those still-water people. Why didn't you *tell* me you knew him?"

Loralei could only stare blankly into Amy's flashing eyes.

"Who?"

"Who? Why, our Mystery Man, of course! That handsome hunk of manhood that keeps appearing and disappearing—and it's *you* he has been meeting all along. Why, you were together in Mazatlan!"

Chapter Four

*L*oralei realized suddenly that the deck around Amy and her was almost deserted. Only a few spectators gathered at the rail to watch the rising breakers. Without warning, a breaker came crashing against the glass wall to fill her face with salt spray and send little rivulets of water coursing down the surface and back to sea. Amy, whose back was to the wall, shrieked, "I could've been washed overboard! Let's get to our room!"

A sudden terror filled Loralei's heart. The little words dropped here and there had been meaningless at the time. But they spelled danger now. There really was a storm at sea. The elevators were packed, so the two girls took the stairs to the Fiesta Deck.

Once inside the cabin, tidied while they were out, Loralei ventured, "What do they do in cases like this?"

"The storm?" Amy shivered as she readied for a shower. "I've never been aboard when one struck. We had a drill before you got on that showed us how to use

life-jackets—which reminds me, I had them bring an extra for you."

The finger that pointed to an upper shelf shook. "You
know, Lory, I'm not afraid to die since I've found my
way back to God, thanks to my special *you*—but I think
it makes a difference where and how!"

Loralei smiled. Then the two of them laughed together,
breaking the tension. "I'm sure the ship's crew will know
how to handle this."

"Wonderful you," Amy said, blowing her a fingertip
kiss and stepping into the bathroom just as the ship rose
and then pitched forward, making the shower curtains
billow out like sails filled with air. Amy grabbed at the
towel bar of the open door.

"Oops! I'd better get that shower over with quickly—
then we'll talk," she said significantly.

But she still hesitated.

"You really *are* wonderful, you know, Loralei—"

"I was thinking the same about you," Loralei said with
a catch in her throat. "Words cannot tell you what your
taking me in has meant. There's no way I can explain—"

"I know—a part of your mystique. You and this mysterious stranger. Oh, it's wonderful! I was in need of excitement and I'm getting it—thanks to you!"

A side roll of the ship caused Amy to drop her towel.
But she didn't seem to notice. Something seemed to be
troubling her and she was having difficulty putting it into words.

"You have a certain power—a certain quality you
don't even know about—I can't put my finger on it—I
know!" Her face lighted. "You're a magical weaver—
that's what you are. You spin life's useless stubble into

rich, gold fabric for us all. No wonder two men are ready to stage a sunrise duel for your hand!"

"Oh, Amy, you don't know what you're saying—"

I mustn't cry. I mustn't. I can't have her suspicious. . . sympathetic. . . leading me to talk of my circumstances. And I can't let her know that things are no longer right between God and me. I can be an actress. I know my lines. I will play my part well. . .

She waited until the vivacious Amy closed the door before bursting into a new flood of tears.

Toweled and glowing, Amy shrugged herself into a striped velveteen mini robe. "Now," she said, sitting down on the vanity stool to brush her hair, "tell me how you came to set up the rendezvous with Mystery Man in Mazatlan!"

"It's not like that, Amy," Loralei said, shaking her head in concentration of what to say next.

Amy was intrigued. "You mean you're going to be as mysterious as *he* is? Not even an *inkling?*"

"It's not the way you think—"

"You don't know the way I'm thinking!"

Loralei knew she must reflect sadness in her answer— sadness mixed with purest joy. How could she explain that concept when it was something she herself didn't understand?

"It doesn't matter what you're thinking, Amy. You couldn't guess the way things are. I wish I could make you understand—"

"Try!"

"There's no way, Amy. I—I'm trying to work my way out of this myself and it's all so—so complicated—" She saw the other girl's quick look of compassion when her voice broke.

"I'm sorry, Lory. Genuinely sorry—I shouldn't have pried—"

"Don't apologize," Loralei said quickly. "I owe you more of an explanation than I can give."

"You owe me nothing. It's the other way around—and, anyway," Amy laid her hair brush down and swept her long hair from her face with a graceful hand, "would you believe that I prayed long and hard that the Lord would send me somebody or something, a *cause,* on this otherwise empty cruise? All I had seen was a crowd of shallow escapees from the prisons they've made of life—running for all it's worth with their backs to the sun! But you're different."

"How?" Loralei wondered what the answer could be.

"Why," Amy said, turning full-face to look into her eyes, "you *face* the sun—letting life's shadows fall behind you!"

Oh, Amy...Jerrod...don't look to me for strength. My well is dry...

While she was still searching for an answer, Amy spoke again. "You are the answer—or part of it. You've changed the atmosphere around here already! And I can ask your advice on the rest—"

Sensing something in the other girl's voice, a kind of loneliness and longing she had never heard before, Loralei said, "What's wrong, Amy? Is something troubling you?"

Amy rose but sank back onto the stool when there was a long rolling motion of the ship cutting a monstrous wave. "Kind of makes one forget about lunch—right? Oh, troubling me, yeah, you might say that. I'm sick to death of a meaningless existence. I have this sudden need to be *needed.* Make sense?"

Loralei nodded and Amy went on, "My folks have no need of me. They're only vaguely aware that they have a daughter. My friends don't credit me with any brains. The men I meet—well, it's either money or physical relationships they pursue from the first eye contact. I'm tired of being wanted for the wrong reasons—such as being an heiress. Do you have any notion of how many oil wells my father owns?"

Loralei shook her head and Amy laughed bitterly. "Neither do I, but it makes no difference. My mother owns the rest!"

A sudden pity and understanding swept over Loralei. Poor little rich girl—rich in everything but what counted. She moved to put a sympathetic hand out but was stopped by another lurch of the ship. By that time Amy was determinedly in control and was speaking in her normal voice.

"If nothing comes my way I may be driven to enter the sisterhood."

"The *what?*"

"Become a nun. You've heard of them?" Amy's voice strove for lightness.

"You have no background for that kind of thing—"

"I can learn!" Amy's jaw jutted out.

"Amy," Loralei said as gently as she knew how, "you're bright. Of course, you could learn. And you've already declared your faith in God and your desire to serve in some way. But listen to me—I don't know much about the kind of field we're discussing, but I feel one thing very deeply in my heart."

"Yes?" With the whispered word, Amy strained toward her.

"Those dedicated sisters aren't *driven* to serve as they

do. I feel that the desire must be very, very strong—so strong that they have sacrificed every earthly thing to become sisters of mercy. Ask yourself if you're ready for that—and then look at the other Amy, the one we know, love, and need, the unique *you*. Then answer the call you hear in your own heart."

Amy bit pensively on the polished nail of her index finger, then idly felt to see if she had broken it before she said softly, "I thank you for that."

And then in her usual bright voice, she said, "And now let's have a look into that bulging closet to see which of the things you like."

As the ship was tossing them back and forth, Amy said with a giggle, "I've had my head banged by that door, skinned a shin, and smashed my nose enough. Here, let's dump the whole deal onto the beds."

Loralei helped lift the clothing off the racks, marveling as she did so at the endless parade of soft chiffons, shimmering velvets, sports coordinates, and loose-fitting casuals. Roz had been right. There was more than enough for three people, but she had reservations.

"What's wrong?" Amy asked, sensing hesitation.

"It's just that I—I don't feel right borrowing these when some haven't ever been worn before."

"Borrowing? Your word, not mine. Once you've worn them, they'll be secondhand—and no daughter of my father's could tarnish the Farrell image like that! Besides," she teased, "I may be entering the convent— or going to some hill to meditate—so *hush!*"

Loralei felt yesterday's nausea returning. It could be from the motion of the ship. Or it could be one of the symptoms the doctor mentioned? Maybe it went with the dizziness and headaches she had told him about. The headaches would worsen...then blindness...but she had run out, closing her ears with her hands. She was unwilling to entertain the thoughts then and she was unwilling now. So in spite of the swaying motion of the ship, she concentrated on the pile of luxuriously-beautiful garments spread before her.

In spite of the futility of it all, Loralei sensed excitement welling up inside when she felt the caress of silk against her skin and heard the whisper of taffeta as Amy all but pushed her through scores of stunning outfits.

"And wait'll you see yourself in this green chiffon!" Amy coaxed even as Loralei protested.

And Amy was right, she realized, surveying herself in the cloud of sea-foam green. The color intensified the green flecks in her eyes, whitened her skin, and added sheen to her hair.

"Oh, Jerrod will love it," Loralei whispered before she realized she was speaking the thoughts in her heart.

"Who?" Amy's eyes were round "O's." "I thought his name was Paul."

Flustered, Loralei felt her words coming out mumbo jumbo. "He—Jerrod—Paul—I—just somebody I know who—who—"

Amy saved the moment by laughing and then Loralei was in control.

"Speaking of names," she said quickly, "does the name Theron Stone mean anything to you?"

"No. Should it?" Amy answered.

Loralei decided to handle the matter lightly. Just why, she didn't know—any more than she knew why it had seemed important not to reveal Jerrod's name.

"Probably not," she said as the two of them began picking up the clothing they had selected for the remainder of the cruise. "I just thought you may have met him during the earlier part of the cruise."

Amy tossed her a jewel box. "Pick out what you want—any or all. It's just costume jewelry. The real stuff's locked in the ship vault. Is this Theron man in the running, too?"

"Oh, Amy, stop that!" Loralei felt herself color. "I don't even know if he's still aboard. Maybe he never was."

Amy hooted. "You know, as long as I've known you I feel like I'm just now getting to *really* know you."

"I think," said Loralei very slowly, "that I am just now getting to know myself."

The ship pitched forward and Loralei felt her senses reel.

"Is it always this rough?" she managed, wondering if she could make it to the bathroom before the next stomach-churning roll.

"You're pea-green—Lory, are you all right? Here, let me help you—"

But Loralei sat down instead. "I think I'll be O.K. It's just that I've never traveled by sea before."

"I'm not buying that excuse altogether," Amy said quietly. "I've had the feeling all along there's something wrong—"

"Nothing's wrong!" Loralei realized she had spoken too quickly and that her voice was sharp. "That's not true," she said more gently. "There is something wrong, but there's nothing you can do except one thing. Please don't push me. Let me think."

"That can be managed, Lory. Now, let's decide what we *can* do. There's a lot going on up top—swimming, deck games, dance classes—and, oh, just wait until the night life begins! Won't you be a knockout tonight in that green chiffon with," she giggled, "Jerrod, Theron, and Paul drawing straws—"

"Paul!"

"Well, maybe not tonight, but soon." Amy turned slowly to face Loralei. "Oh, Lory, maybe I did something awful. The purser stopped me and gave me Paul's cablegram and I thought how romantic it would be if he joined you aboard ship—have I done something wrong?"

"What have you done?" Loralei whispered through frozen lips.

"I read the message before I realized it wasn't mine. I knew you were in love with this Golden Boy and when I saw that question, 'Your place or mine?' I—well, I wired back and said, 'Mine!' Do you think he'll come—was he serious?"

When Loralei could only moan, Amy sprang to her quickly and, squatting beside her on the bed, buried her dark head in Loralei's lap. "Oh, Lory, forgive me—forgive me—I'm so sorry!"

Loralei stroked the girl's long hair gently. *I am, too, Amy,* her heart cried out. *I am, too...*

Amy insisted that the two of them go to the dining room for the one o'clock sitting. Nothing worse for seasickness than an empty stomach. The mention of food set Loralei's stomach churning all the more. She wanted to be alone to sort out her thoughts. Roz, however, bounced in to change clothes after tennis. So there would be no privacy. Her news did away with all hope of solitude, replacing it with a very real fear.

"We're on the edge of a terrible storm. There's a full-blown hurricane between us and—would you believe?—San Diego. At least, they think it might go ashore. Winds.

Torrential rain. Rumor has it that we may have to turn
back to Mazatlan. No harbor at Cabo San Lucas, you
know—''

The three of them could only look at each other in
white-faced terror as Roz answered questions and they
hazarded guesses as to what would happen once they were
back in Mazatlan's harbor.

Part of Loralei listened to the words the other two girls
were saying. Another part was wondering what had happened to the world of the sane...where people went
back and forth to work every day...ate and slept on
schedule—and planned for a cozy retirement with the person they loved.

And with that thought came another. Jerrod! She had
to see him. Be with him. None of this mattered. None
of it at all...but supposing she had dreamed it all—even
Jerrod? A knife twisted inside her heart at the thought
and, even though the ship was pitching crazily from side
to side, she made her way to the vanity dresser for
reassurance. Hoping Amy and Roz were not looking,
Loralei let her fingers close around the metal object in
front of her.

Oh, blessed assurance! *The key*...so Jerrod had to be
real. A dream, no matter how beautiful, could never leave
a key! Her illness hadn't caused hallucinations...

In the dining room Loralei tried to concentrate on the
menu. She would try to get some soup down to keep from
being sick. But what kind would the lady wish? The waiter
hovered to point out the long list. Who cared about soup?
Bring her anything, Loralei told the disappointed waiter.
Then she let her eyes wander over the dining room in
search of the hauntingly wonderful face of the man she
loved.

"He's not here," Amy said suddenly causing Loralei to jump. Then, turning to Roz who was eating heartily on the full-course lunch, Amy asked, "Have you seen our Mystery Man?"

Roz, pushing away a glistening avocado appetizer as if it were a foreign food, did not look up.

"Yes," she said excitedly, "and guess what! He was talking with a man in plain clothes who was flashing a badge. Suppose he's a secret agent?"

"More likely a movie star traveling incognito to avoid fans," Amy offered.

"Depend on you Californians to come up with *that* reason—and to be able to attack an avocado with zest! But Mystery Man has no friends as far as I can see—"

"Oh, but he does—" Amy caught herself in time and clapped a rosy-tipped finger to her lip. "I mean, *I* think he would have at least one."

The bad moment passed and Loralei continued to scan the diners one by one, searching every face, while her companions swapped travel talk about passengers they had made a game of trying to identify. But Jerrod was not there.

Amy and Roz finished full meals while Loralei toyed with her soup. They wanted to take a spin around the deck, storm or no storm, but Loralei declined their invitation to join them. Slippery footing of the deck would be more than she could cope with right now.

Most of the diners were gone, but the waiter insisted on bringing her a cup of hot tea.

"It will help to settle your stomach, lovely lady, and there are some rough seas ahead."

Idly, Loralei squeezed a wedge of lemon into the amber liquid. The lights dimmed and the room grew quiet. She was unaware that someone had eased into the chair opposite her until a strong, familiar hand reached out to capture both of hers.

"Jerrod," she whispered without daring to look up.

His voice was as shaken as hers when he breathed, "Loralei—Loralei darling, I found you!"

Chapter Five

*L*oralei had no idea how long she and Jerrod sat, hands clasped across the table. Neither of them spoke, but it was a time of magic. Loralei wished there were a "Lost and Found" for ideas. She had spent every waking hour thinking of words to say that would express her feelings, questions she would ask—not prying ones, for details didn't matter, just those that would tell her how long they had together.

But the words were lost. And suddenly it no longer mattered. Eyes locked together as theirs were spoke the language of the heart. *Somehow, somewhere we'll be together,* Jerrod's eyes promised tenderly. And in that enchanting moment, she believed it was true.

The white-coated waiter crumbed the table nervously the first time he came, breaking the spell of silence. Would they like something more? he wondered the second time. Then the third time the dapper little man touched a pencil-thin moustache and whispered discretely,

"We will be leaving the dining room, but if you would like a bit of forbidden privacy, yes? Then there's a little alcove—" And he pointed to a small upper-level corner where a large porthole overlooked the sea.

Jerrod thanked him, reached a hand to help Loralei from the table, and put his arm securely around her for support while the red-carpeted floor seemed to heave and sigh as if writhing in pain. Together they made their way to the secluded spot. Each time Loralei's feet faltered, Jerrod tightened his grip, his lean arm strong and warm against her back, his hand encircling her waist so far that the fingers of his left arm seemed to span it completely. She was warm. Secure. Unafraid. Together, they could change what they could. Together, they would bear the rest...

"It's a bad storm, isn't it, Jerrod?" Loralei asked at last.

"It's bad," Jerrod said, "but don't be afraid, Lory." His hands tightened over hers across the table.

Loralei shook her head and together they looked out the porthole. The water had changed from its tranquil blue to angry green. Breakers that seemed intent on destroying the ship rose higher than the vessel, broke, and emptied their fury on the deserted decks. The sky was near-black with towering banks of clouds.

And yet, somehow there was an eerie feeling of stillness above them as if the storm were waiting for them to cross an invisible line which only it knew.

Loralei shivered in spite of herself and turned from the porthole.

"Are we headed back to Mazatlan?"

"Not yet, but there's talk of it. Don't worry, Lory. Just enjoy the moment."

Loralei squeezed the hands that held hers with all her strength. "Oh, Jerrod, I love you. I—I love you. You do love *me?*" She raised a stricken face, knowing that her heart was in her eyes.

Jerrod groaned.

"How can you ask? I love you with all my heart. You are what I have searched for all my life." His voice was as choked with emotion as her own.

Then Loralei asked the age-old question of a woman in love. "For how long, Jerrod? How long have you known?"

Jerrod's laugh was low and deep. But there was pain in it, too. Pain that perhaps only she would recognize because of her own.

"I have loved you before you knew me. I've always known *you.*"

Somebody had loved her before she knew him. But he had always known her. Somehow the words had a familiar ring—one that was disturbingly comforting.

But, no! She was not going to fall into that kind of thinking. It was a trap. She wanted to believe there was Someone looking out for her, loving her, taking care. But it all fell apart like a spun-glass ornament, smashing the false beauty it had created...

"Lory, what is it? You look as if you had seen a ghost." There was concern in Jerrod's tender eyes.

"It's nothing—" And then, because she was unable to help herself, Loralei felt the words torn from her, "Oh, Jerrod, how long do we have?"

He inhaled deeply. His breath seemed to catch in a sigh, but his voice, when he spoke, was strong.

"This week," he said, "unless—no, let's just say this week or what remains of it. I flew to Acapulco and boarded ship while some of the other passengers will cruise both ways. Of course, with this storm—"

"But if the storm lets up?"

"Well, we were to get into Cabo San Lucas today. From there to San Diego—bypassing it—and on to Los Angeles. But, then, you already knew that." He looked at her questioningly.

Loralei shook her head.

"I don't know anything about the itinerary," she explained.

She told him then how she came to be on the cruise. No details. No inkling of how she came to be in Mazatlan or that it was by accident that she met up with Amy. Simply that she had met up with a friend and was sharing quarters—

At Jerrod's quick look, Loralei gave a little laugh.

"A *girl* friend," she assured him. "My roommate from college."

But Jerrod did not laugh. He did not even smile.

"There is nobody else then? You are not married—or engaged?"

"Married, no. I was engaged, but—"

The ship rocked dangerously and for one frightening moment seemed about to turn on its side. In that dark moment, Loralei left her sentence unfinished.

"You have a right to ask the same questions of me, Lory—or do you know the answers?" Jerrod inquired when the danger was past.

"I know all I need to know. I know that you are troubled—"

Jerrod's eyes took on the haunted look she remembered from Mazatlan.

"And I know the same about you. But I think we both

know neither of our troubles can be resolved by talking about them.''

She nodded miserably. And Jerrod continued, ''But I'll tell you that my company sent me on the cruise as a little bonus for ideas I had developed for World Wide Computers. I didn't deserve it!''

The last sentence was bitter—the first bitterness she had heard in his voice.

''Oh, I'm sure you did—and more! That wonderful idea you shared in the little church—about the bells—''

''Just a dream, my darling,'' Jerrod's voice was low-pitched and intimate again.

''But you'll be going back to it—making it come true,'' Loralei began eagerly.

''No!'' The bitterness again. And then more gently Jerrod whispered, ''Do you realize, my darling, how much time we are wasting on tomorrows when we should be basking in the beauty of this day—the only moments we can be sure of?''

Tears welled up in Loralei's heart and moved from there to her eyes. With an aching throat, she nodded.

''Then let's cherish every moment—every star-studded second of this golden hour. It isn't as if I could reach out, take you in my arms and ask the question I want with all my heart to ask. I have no future to offer you.''

Loralei's words were almost inaudible, but she saw by the look on Jerrod's tormented face that he had heard.

''I couldn't accept that future, Jerrod. You're right—we have only this day.''

''No more talking then—not ever—about what lies ahead.''

Then, with their hands clenched together until the knuckles showed white, they looked at the churning sea again. Storms had always frightened Loralei, but this one was beautiful in its fury, its majesty, its power to move an ocean. Any storm, like last night's sunset and this morning's sunrise, could be her last. And even if perchance she survived the two years the doctor had given her, there would be no Jerrod.

So it didn't matter. Quantity of years lost their meaning. Only quality counted now.

"Oh, Jerrod, Jerrod, I love you!" she burst out in joy of the here-and-now.

Almost savagely then Jerrod drew her hands to his lips, uncurled the fingers, and kissed her palms over and over. At last, he drew her hands up to cover his face completely and spoke brokenly, his voice muffled by her palms.

"Store these in the hope chest of your heart, Lory, little sweetheart. They're all we have."

And when he released her hands, she saw that they were wet like her own cheeks. Oh, how could God be so cruel?

"Some day we'll understand," Jerrod promised, his words strangely convincing in tone.

Only she wouldn't, of course. Never in a million years!

The hour must have grown late. Shadows gathered around them in a way that made togetherness more intimate. Candles in the squat, little lanterns flickered with the rolling of the ship to send fingers of light across Jerrod's face, illuminating his eyes with an other-worldly shine.

Fascinated, Loralei watched the lights and, never letting her gaze drop from his, allowed herself to drown in the sea of his loving eyes.

He was Adam. She was Eve. They were in a newly-created world still rocked in a chaos of hot, new seas

separating themselves to let the land bodies emerge. Sin
had not yet entered the world. And they, the innocents,
were alone in the Garden's leafy bower... *oh, Jerrod!*

"Tell me about yourself, Lory," Jerrod said softly. "I
gave you no chance to talk in Mazatlan."

Loralei felt her shyness returning. She wanted to concentrate on Jerrod, not on herself. "There's nothing to
tell," she said. "I'm so ordinary." Then, in an attempt
at lightness, she added, "I stand five-seven-and-a-half
barefoot and weigh 105 pounds soaking wet—"

"—walk like a queen, are exquisitely beautiful, and are
delightfully unaware of it all," Jerrod finished for her.
"All this I know and much, much more, plus how much
I love you—but I'm not sure you even told me where you
lived. Or do we skip that?"

I won't LIVE anywhere very long, my darling... but
aloud she told him about Santa Monica, the name sounding foreign to her lips in this strange, new world. An
only child, she had lost both parents. Her job paid little
but was fun. Ambitions? None really—unless one could
count dreams.

And suddenly she was saying too much. About wanting a home. Children. To grow daffodils in the spring-
time. Make old-fashioned apple jelly in the fall. Love and
be loved. And, inspired by it all, when her husband had
gone to work—happy and well-fed—and the children,
stuffed with hot oatmeal, had settled down for naps, she
would paint her world as she saw it. A virtual paradise!

With a little gasp, Loralei stopped. But it was Jerrod
who gave a low moan of pain.

"I can't enter that picture, Loralei—but, like you told
me about the bells, hang onto the dream. It's right for
you."

Loralei shook her head, closing her eyes to hide the tears.

"No, Jerrod. It can never be now. I can't talk about it—please understand," she pleaded. "But understand that it no longer matters because I wouldn't want it without you."

The waiters began to move quietly among the tables in preparation for dinner. *"La Nuit Francaise,"* the menu said. Having forgotten that there was an audience in the alcove, the men spoke of the storm. Everything must be made normal, they said, to avoid panic among the passengers. Bright lights...here string them here...swags above each table...mimosa, great bouquets of mimosa, in the center...the sturdier crystal in case the ship's lurching upset the tables. Yes, they would be turning back. But soon enough? Who knew?

In a dream, Loralei heard. It was simply another chapter of a book she was reading.

"Now, my love," Jerrod said suddenly as he picked up a menu, "what will you have? First, an appetizer. Les escargots bourguignonne, la quiche lorraine, les poireaux vinaigrette—or all?"

Loralei felt a ripple of laughter touch her lips.

"I don't know a word of French."

Jerrod twirled an imaginary moustache. "Ah, then I will translate, my cheri! Baked snails, no? Savory egg custard—or perhaps leeks with vinegar dressing—unless, my cheri wishes to skip this course and wander down the dark corridors with her admirer?" He leaned forward, "Before we are beheaded!"

Giggling, the two of them held hands and crept stealthily toward the door like stowaways. When they had reached pretended safety, Jerrod reached for her. But the ship gave a sudden roll and clumsily she fell into his arms. His kiss missed her lips and landed on her nose. Then they laughed. Less at the incident than for the sheer joy of being together. Together was where they belonged. Forever and ever. Around them there would always be laughter. Other people would light up in their presence . . .

In the crowded elevator, they clung close together, not minding at all. The others seemed edgy and upstairs the games, heretofore leisurely, were frenzied. Passengers knotted in little groups, gravitating together as if there were safety in numbers.

Loralei hardly noticed. She and Jerrod moved in a world all their own. In the lobby, Jerrod picked up a copy of *Love Notes,* a little newsletter published daily at sea. Skimming past the weather and summary of the world news, he read aloud, " 'Formal dress tonight.' Is there room for me at your table?"

Before thinking, Loralei said, "Oh, then you're going to the dining room?"

Jerrod looked at her strangely and there was no way of telling him that her roommates had discussed his not being there before. But he recovered quickly and the awkward moment passed.

"Tonight, yes—and what are you wearing?"

"A sea-foam green dress," she said quickly. The most beautiful thing Amy had shared from her extravagant wardrobe. Oh, she had to be beautiful for Jerrod! And something else—some inner voice—seemed to be prompting Loralei to say, "The time is now."

Her father, she remembered, had lived in Tomorrow's World. No time for his wife and daughter. That would come when he retired. Only Tomorrow never came. And

Mother—well, Mother had lived in Yesterday's World. Remembering her courtship with Loralei's father, *living* in it because there was no Today, no Tomorrow.

Look what happened to Mother...only somehow the thought no longer made her sad. Instead, Loralei felt a certain appreciation that she herself had come to know how precious Today's World could be. When time with someone you loved was limited. When life itself, like time with that person, was sifting out grain by grain through an hourglass that was invisible to the human eye.

So caught up in thoughts that she was unaware of her surroundings, Loralei was suddenly overwhelmed by the headiness of a million blossoms that seemed to close in on her from all directions. Roses. Carnations. Marigolds. Those she could identify. But they were hothouse plants and tattled the process of forced growth. Over and above their falseness came the overpowering sweetness of flowers that smelled of sunshine, air, and life.

Jasmine! Real jasmine, the kind she remembered in her grandmother's Southern home. Gram'ma called it "yellow jassamine" because of its light color. The vines trailed along the eaves and wove around her heart, but never, ever had she hoped to see or smell their fragrance again.

They were in the ship's florist shop, Loralei realized, and Jerrod was talking to the middle-aged keeper.

"They are what I want," he said insistently. He broke off a waxy blossom and handed it to Loralei. She inhaled deeply, wanting the memory to linger forever.

"Yes," she said softly, "oh, yes, this is what we must have!"

"How much?"

But the lady was protesting. "These are not for sale,

sir!" She moved her square body between him and the buckets of wild flowers. "They're not for corsages. Most inappropriate. These are for tonight's decorations and— well, for me to allow them to go would be out of the question unless there were extenuating circumstances."

"I see," Jerrod said thoughtfully. "Is this an extenuating circumstance?"

The bill he handed her must have been large. She backed away from the buckets, scooped up an armful of the blossom-strung vines, and reached for the green florist tissue.

The storm no longer mattered as Loralei buried her face in the sweet fragrance of the jasmine. The ship rocked from side to side so that Jerrod had to hold onto the brass railing with one hand, supporting her with the other.

Outside, Loralei was sure the wind was demon-driven. The sky would be black with forboding. But to Loralei it was turquoise velvet, strewn with every star in the firmament, reflecting the glory of dancing lights along the golden shore of some beckoning island.

The song of the water against the ship was soft, washing the image of the stars against the sides. And over it all lay a heavy layer of jasmine...

Turning to Jerrod with a little open-mouthed gasp of total surrender, she whispered to him.

"I can't resist the moment—fight though I will. Oh, Jerrod, I'm glad we happened to meet and fall in love— even though it's a transient happiness—I will always be glad—"

Jerrod met her mouth halfway.

"No happiness is ever transient, my darling—it stores in the heart," he murmured between kisses.

Purest joy encompassed the two of them. The ageless, timeless kind of happiness that knows no beginning and no end. They wouldn't exchange addresses when the cruise ended—either by shipwreck or on schedule—and they would never exchange vows. But they had the present.

They clung to each other almost desperately. When at last Jerrod released her, shaken and his eyes lit with sadness and joy, Loralei laughed shakily.

"I'll do well to get myself beautiful for you. Help me to my cabin."

Jerrod held tightly to her and she held on fast to the great bouquet of wild jasmine. At the door of her suite, he said, "Shall I come for you at eight-thirty?"

"No, I'll meet you in the dining room. O.K.?"

As she raised her eyes to his, Loralei was sure she saw a man's eyes studying the two of them. Then when she caught his eye, he slipped quickly around the corner of the cabin at the far end of the narrow hall.

The eyes were familiar. Where—and then it came back to her. He was the man—a Captain Max Avery, wasn't it?—who asked her the questions.

Sight of him made her uneasy. She had everything in order now. Her passport. A place to stay. What could he want with her—unless he still thought she knew something about that man—

"Jerrod," she said suddenly, "who is Theron Stone?"

Did she imagine Jerrod suck his breath in sharply? Probably, for his voice was normal when he spoke.

"One of my colleagues—but how did you—"

He paused and then let his breath out as if relieved. "Oh, of course! His initials are on my attache case. I borrowed it."

That explained nothing. But why burden Jerrod with her concerns? And only later did Loralei realize that the initials "T.S." would not have revealed to her that they stood for Theron Stone...that Jerrod was indeed covering something up. That he, not she, was watched.

Chapter Six

*L*oralei had the quarters to herself and was able to dress with care. Roz had suffered an acute attack of seasickness, her first, and was in the infirmary. Amy, interested in a special floor show, had exchanged seatings with another passenger and was dining early. Like a schoolgirl, she dressed excitedly.

In spite of the rolling of the ship, Loralei was able to survey herself in the mirror and her reflection was more than reassuring. She had never looked more beautiful. Of that she was certain. Amy was right. The frothy chiffon was perfect for her. The ruffles at the neckline broke the simplicity of the princess lines—a style which revealed a figure Loralei had never suspected she possessed.

Maybe the green of the material emphasized the highlights in her eyes, but she suspected that love was more likely responsible. And the same for the glow of her skin. Who needed a blusher? A touch of lip gloss, the slippers that looked like Cinderella's glass ones, and a final brush and fluff of the wispy bangs across her forehead. And she was ready just as the gong sounded and the deep voice announced, "Main seating in the dining room now in progress. Bon appetit!"

At the door, she paused and with a smile turned back to the dressing table. There, from the enormous vase where she had placed the jasmine, Loralei plucked a spray and held it experimentally against her face. The effect and the heady odor were irresistible. With a song in her heart, she swept her hair behind her right ear and pinned the creamy blossoms so that they brushed her cheek. It was to be an evening to remember forever.

Jerrod, handsome in his stark black and white, waited at the door of the Continental Dining Room. Loralei saw him before he noticed her. She watched his grave eyes searching every face, their depths lighted with anticipation.

How different he was from the other men aboard who were taking this voyage simply because they were bored with life. But then he was different from all other men in the world—

Their eyes met then, his deep gray ones and her green-flecked ones, melting together like their hearts. Three long strides brought him to her. He reached for her hand, squeezed it, and led her to the ornately trellised wall the ship's crew had improvised at the table she shared with the other two girls.

Fleetingly, she wondered where Jerrod's table was and then forgot it in the sheer joy of their being together.

"You look like something lovely from another century," Jerrod said tenderly. "So untouched by the world—and tonight you are!"

The wine steward came to offer a menu, but Jerrod dismissed him with a shake of his head. From somewhere there came the soft, haunting strains of Parisian music. Above the sad-sweet voice of the violins, Loralei said, "It's amazing how our tastes and values are so similar."

Jerrod smiled and concentrated on the menu. But she concentrated on his face. She must remember every detail to carry with her, to have and to hold for whatever remained of life, and even—yes—to cherish on Death's narrow bed.

Tearing her eyes away from Jerrod's face in an effort to stem the tears that threatened, Loralei's eyes met the eyes of another man head-on. Coldly and with calculation, the commanding dark eyes were watching from a dissipated face of a man who appeared to be in his late sixties.

Involuntarily, Loralei let out a low cry.

Jerrod dropped the menu.

"What is it, Loralei? What's wrong, my darling?"

"That man—the one with the high pompadour—"

Jerrod looked in the direction where she moved her head. But the man was gone.

Loralei shivered and reached for her fringed shawl. Jerrod rose from the table to help her, his eyes panning the dining room as he stood.

She would remember the awful eyes of the stranger forever. But by the time Jerrod eased his great height back into the chair opposite her, she was in control of her emotions again.

She was even able to respond with a smile when Jerrod suggested that the man undoubtedly was envying him. But she shook her head when he added, "Nobody could gaze upon you tonight without admiration!"

"It wasn't admiration," Loralei said slowly. "It was—I don't know what it was—but this isn't the first time strange things have happened today."

And then, without having planned to, Loralei was telling him about catching glimpses of men who seemed to be watching her and her one encounter with the F.B.I. agent. Jerrod looked alarmed, even more so than she had expected. His face had even changed color during her explanation.

"You mean he interrogated you and never explained why?"

"I don't understand it, but yes, he did."

A look of anger crossed Jerrod's face then. It changed him completely and the metamorphosis was almost frightening. His eyes were dark with fury—or was it fear? A mixture of both. She regretted having upset him. And surely they were making too much of the incidents. Maybe they were routine.

Jerrod leaned toward her.

"If any of the men contact you again, I want to know about it, Loralei. They have no right!"

"Oh, Jerrod, I'm sorry. I shouldn't have upset you. It's all my fault. There was some question about—well, about the circumstances of my being here maybe—" she stumbled on miserably.

Jerrod dropped his head almost to his chest and a low moan escaped from his pale lips.

"It's no fault of yours, Lory darling. It has nothing to do with you—oh, I wish we had parted in Mazatlan for keeps—that we had not met again—or, better, that we had never met. You shouldn't be dragged in on this!"

"Dragged in, Jerrod? I don't understand."

"I know you don't. And that's what hurts. But *you're*

not under surveillance. *I* am!'' Defeat underscored every word.

She had known all along that something was wrong. It made no sense then. It made no sense now. And it made no difference in their lives! She had to make Jerrod see that.

''Jerrod,'' she said in a low, agonized whisper, ''I am being watched, too—oh, not the way you are maybe—'' she added when his head shot up, ''but watched just the same.''

Loralei paused then, wondering if she could get another word past the rock in her throat.

Death's Angel stalks my every footstep, she mused silently, *his sardonic grin reminding me to count my every breath.*

But this, like Jerrod's secret, was private. Neither had anything to offer the other—except this night, this hour, this moment. They must not let it pass.

Then she took a long shot. Maybe a wrong one, she thought. But worth it.

''Jerrod,'' she said, feeling her tongue thick in her mouth with the deceptive words. ''You told me back in the little church that you had faith in God.''

Jerrod's hands gripped hers so hard that she felt as if the knuckles were cracking, that blood was oozing from her nailtips just as it oozed from her heart.

''I'm not putting on a very good demonstration, am I?''

''We all have to be reminded sometimes—''

Jerrod interrupted, his voice stronger now.

''Do you trust me, Loralei?''

''Unconditionally,'' she said, putting her heart into her words.

"Then you have helped me reach a decision—realize what I have to do. And after that—"

When he stopped in mid-sentence, his eyes probed deeply into hers. Loralei saw that they had lost some of their haunted look.

"After that," Jerrod repeated, italicizing every word, *"we will talk about that future we thought was impossible!"*

The waiter brought cold cucumber soup and Loralei was able to postpone the inevitable. . .the moment when she must tell Jerrod that nothing he could do would give them a future together.

The waiter seemed to linger interminably. Would they like orange sauce with the roast duckling? And curacao liqueur, no? Perhaps mixed green salad with walnuts—and, of course, coffee.

When at length the tall man in the white coat folded his napkin over his arm and marched away, Loralei turned back to Jerrod. The happiness that glowed there cut her more deeply than the pain she had seen before. And it was she who must destroy it.

"Jerrod—" she toyed with her silver. "Jerrod, this is hard for me, but there is something—something I must say. And once I say it, you must not question me. I—I can't talk about it—I—I—oh, Jerrod, there is no future for us. No matter what you have decided. You see, *I* have no future."

And then, in spite of her effort to be brave, Loralei snatched her hands from Jerrod's. Burying her face in them, she burst into tears that wracked her body.

I am making a scene, she thought wildly, *something I have never done before in my life! LIFE! Oh, why must that word crop up in every breath I take?*

"Move over!" Jerrod was at her side, pushing himself into the seat beside her. She was in his arms, aware only of their great strength and the fragrance of jasmine as he cradled her head against his shoulder.

"Make it all right. Make it all right!" she whispered, not sure whether her words were a prayer or a plea with the man who was trying to protect her from the pre-ordained.

"Loralei, I have a plan—"

But before Jerrod could complete his sentence bells began to ring and the ship's whistles cut through the air. There was a crackle of static on the loudspeaker and the ship seemed to have stalled at sea. All merriment ceased. Even the storm seemed to hold its breath. A feeling of impending disaster dimmed the lights, reducing them to their artificiality. With gaping mouths, the diners all waited.

"This is your captain speaking." The voice was controlled but carried no reassurance. "I regret to be the bearer of bad tidings, but it is necessary that there be a change in plans—"

Some of his next words were lost in static, then lost again in the little gasps from all over the room and the obvious hysterics of one woman at a back table.

Loralei strained to hear along with Jerrod. The storm was rapidly developing into a full-blown hurricane, the captain said, his voice with its clipped British accent trying to maintain lightness but sounding more like an announcement of doom's day just ahead.

The ship's motors were cut and she was making as wide a sweep as was practical so that starboard side would remain windward with a westerly course leading on to Cabo San Lucas. No disembarkation would be allowed due to the storm. But the tourists stranded there would embark, rough waters allowing.

The captain hoped nobody was disappointed and wished to reassure them that turning their "ship home" toward Mazatlan was only a matter of precaution. No immediate danger. But comfort of passengers was utmost in the minds of the luxury liner's employees, and since there was no port at Cabo San Lucas and the path of the storm was such that perhaps they would be more comfortable in more stable waters...

Well, the captain was sure they understood. And, meantime, what an opportunity to see the ordinarily peaceful Pacific having a bloody bit of a tantrum! Activities would resume. Different. But exciting. And, again, there was no cause for alarm. None!

There was a wild scramble in the dining room. In detached fascination, Loralei watched. How quickly the other passengers became dehumanized—scrambling, shoving, trampling if need be on their fellowmen to get *some*where.

"Their behavior is unbelievable," she said softly almost to herself.

But Jerrod heard.

"Oh, how thin the veneer of what some choose to call 'faith' until there is a test."

"But that's when we need it most," Loralei found herself saying. "Isn't it a last gasp for some?"

Jerrod smiled.

"Maybe," he said softly, "it's because they don't have a *you*."

"Oh, Jerrod—" Loralei tried to protest, but he was not listening.

"All a person has to do to see the stars is look up. But

the view's best when one is flat on his back. And then
it took you to point them out to me. Now the sackcloth
sky above us is so crystal clear that Jeanette McDonald
could destroy it with a single musical note!''

Loralei knew then that she could not destroy the moment. It belonged to her. To Jerrod. And to a Power
greater than either of them.

''I love you,'' she whispered as the crowds jostled by.
''You are the only really good thing that has ever happened to me. I don't want it to end.''

''It isn't going to,'' Jerrod replied confidently. Then,
seeing that the dining room was emptied of people, he
motioned to one of the startled waiters.

''The lady and I are ready to order dessert,'' he in-
formed him.

The ship's engines paused, seemed to reverse momentarily, and then were silent. Through the porthole beside
their table, Loralei and Jerrod watched as through the
slanting sheets of rain a little glimmer of light appeared
in the distance. Harbor lights, only there was no harbor.
The crew would make an attempt to drop anchor, lower
a lifeboat, and go for passengers. It would be perilous
at best—if possible at all, Loralei thought as she looked
at the wind-driven waves which were reaching higher than
the great ship's smokestacks.

''You haven't touched your la coupe aux marrons,''
Jerrod chided gently to bring her eyes away from the
stormy sea.

Loralei looked at the generous scoops of ice cream in
tall crystal parfait glasses, the top glazed with whole
chestnuts and caramel sauce. *It must contain 1,000
calories,* but she did not care.

Giddy with the joy of the moment, she picked up her

spoon, sampled the goodness of the gourmet dish, then laid the spoon down to lace her hands through Jerrod's. His hands were warm with the blood that coursed through them. A warmth she would remember when these precious moments were gone. A touchless touching of two hearts—

Her thoughts were broken by an explosive noise. The ship shuddered. And somewhere there were screams. Then all was quiet. But the dining room looked strange. Chandeliers hung at angles. Tables and chairs had skidded crazily. It was like a dream. Lights burned properly, but something had gone wrong with gravity. That part of the dream was a nightmare. But Jerrod was there with her. And that, to Loralei, made the dream wonderful.

"Eat your dessert," Jerrod ordered, his voice low and coaxing. Then, after she had taken a delicious bite, he shattered her world—made the dream a true nightmare.

"Lory, keep eating," he whispered. "Act normal. There is no storm. No danger. And there are no men standing at the door watching!"

Obediently, Loralei spooned her dessert to her mouth. Carefully. Not too rapidly. Not too slowly. Just normally. Two people enjoying the end of a beautiful meal.

But her heart beat a wild tattoo against her rib cage. Whatever trouble Jerrod was in was drawing to a climax, and something told her that their time together would be even more brief than she had thought.

It was a race as to which of their problems would terminate the once-in-a-lifetime love affair, and his was winning. Soon now it would end. They would be torn apart, and friends would sooth, "Just another shipboard romance. But how exciting!"

"Loralei!" There was a note of desperation in Jerrod's voice. But there was strength in the way he said her name. "What I am about to say will hurt and surprise you. But keep on with your dessert and—eyes down—just listen to what I say!"

Terrified already, she nodded her consent.

"There's something I must do, Lory—a contact I must make. It's doubtful if I could get a cablegram through. Even so, it wouldn't be safe..." Jerrod seemed to be debating with himself, "to communicate from the ship. So—"

If only she could help!

"Tell me, Jerrod. Maybe I can do something. At least, share with me."

"There's no time, my darling. I've been discovered—I mean, they've discovered the shortage—"

"*Shortage?*" Loralei's lips would hardly move in their tightness. "You mean a shortage at your business? The company knew where you were—but the others. Who *are* they—what do they want?"

Funds. Jerrod took money.

The words ran before her eyes as if they were printed upon the walls of the swaying ship. But the moving words made no sense. Jerrod was no thief. He was a valuable employee. Thieves didn't earn bonus trips like this cruise when they dipped into company funds.

Oh, how had this misunderstanding come about? But his next words told her that there *was* no misunderstanding.

"I left a note telling WCC I took the money."

"But that makes no sense, Jerrod." Loralei leaned forward desperately. Only suddenly it did. "You *wanted* to be found. Why, then, did you come—*why,* Jerrod?"

He glanced casually toward the door.

"A delaying tactic."

And when she would have asked more, Jerrod planted a kiss on his right forefinger and placed it to her lips gently.

"No more talking—just your trust in us—in our future—in what I am about to do. I am going to make an attempt to go ashore at Cabo San Lucas—"

"Oh, Jerrod, no!" And, forgetting his instructions, she raised stricken eyes to his face. Immediately, she dropped her gaze. But not before she caught sight of Max Avery and the gray-haired man whose calculating eyes had followed her earlier in the evening.

"They're watching, Jerrod. You could never get away without being detected. And even if you did, you would be drowned—"

Her voice, in spite of all efforts to behave normally, ended in a piteous cry.

"Whatever it is, my darling, don't run anymore! We'll face it—it makes no difference—it *couldn't*—oh, Jerrod!"

Gently, Jerrod caught and held her desperate hands as she reached out to him. Then, for a fleeting second, he allowed his forefinger to trace the base of the third finger of her left hand.

"The ring which spells *eternity* will go there when this is all over—"

"No!" The cry wrenched from her throat said more than he knew. It begged Jerrod not to take the risk . . . to stay with her in the time they had left . . . give her his every moment until these men or the storm claimed them both.

But it said more. Even if he listened to her pleas and stayed, it was just a temporary reprieve. There was no hope for the two of them. No future. "Until death . . ." was but a mockery . . .

The great ship seemed to right itself suddenly. The shudder must have been the dropping of the anchor, Loralei thought dully. Jerrod rose from the table, reached for her hand and pulled her close to whisper a message.

"Be prepared the minute I let you go, Lory. We'll head for the closed door, bypassing our uninvited guests!"

She did as he said and the two of them scurried through the opposite door, catching the men by surprise, she was sure.

Jerrod tried to help her to her room, but she refused to go. Instead, she clung to his hand as with the speed of a cheetah he sprang up the stairs. And suddenly they were on the storm-battered deck, holding onto the rail for support.

Neither of them wore a hat and Loralei's only protection was the lightweight, fringed shawl. Water was ankle-deep. She felt the soft fullness of her green chiffon skirt swish around her legs, clinging to her body like a wet suit. The scarf flew from her shoulders and her hair, rain-drenched, plastered to her face making it almost impossible to see the crewmen at the edge of the deck as they struggled to lower the lifeboat into the churning waters.

Lightning split the sky in half. And in its eerie glow she saw two men in black slickers coming toward them. She tried to scream. But one of the men restrained her, tore her hand from Jerrod's, and dragged her back into the garish lights of the inside hall.

"Jerrod, Jerrod!" she screamed above the shriek of the storm. But the wind sucked her breath away through the open door.

There was only the hollow echo of her swishing foot-steps as the man beside her dragged her along the cor-ridor leading to a door marked *Private.*

The captain's quarters. No, no, she mustn't go there. Not now! She had to make this man understand before it was too late.

Desperately, she turned to him, trying to communicate, say something—*anything*—that would win him to her side. Or at least delay encounter with those who might question her.

"Please—*please*—listen to me. I'll give you no more trouble. Help me to my room. Here is my key."

As yet, Loralei had been unable to see the face hidden by the dripping rain hat. The hat was peaked in front and back, dipping downward to give the impression of a giant black vulture. And she noticed that the man was shaking his head helplessly from side to side.

With a sinking heart, she realized that he was a member of the ship's crew—undoubtedly one of the young men hired from Afghanistan who spoke no English.

Finally, to her enormous relief, he accepted the key. It was necessary for them to turn back to the elevators to go to the floor of her suite. In turning, she caught a glimpse of the heavy glass doors which had blown closed by the wind, their surface drenched by rain. Somewhere out there the darkness had swallowed Jerrod like the Ser-pent of Sin that entered the lives of all who would try to live in their private Eden.

That's the way life is, she thought bitterly. *One tastes the fruit, forbidden but too sweet to deny, and is driven from the Garden. Then comes a second blessing, sweeter than before, a glimpse into the Promised Land. Only one can never enter because of previous sins...*

The crew member struggled with her key. It was a tricky key, she had learned, but she knew how to insert it just right. Loralei could have helped but didn't.

Any move, even the few steps into her room, took her farther away from Jerrod. So why rush, even if she could?

A note which had been propped against Loralei's hair brush had fallen to the floor. She picked it up, finding strange pleasure that the clothes she wore were making widening puddles of discoloring saltwater on the carpet and that her skin was chafing from exposure. Her surroundings needed to be ugly; her body needed to suffer. Unfeelingly, she opened the note. Amy had gone to a late movie. Roz was still in the infirmary. And (big joke!), Amy hoped Loralei hadn't drowned her problems "either at the bar or by jumping overboard!"

Amy would have no idea of the reality of that statement.

Hardly aware of her motions, Loralei took a hot shower and got herself into a nightgown and into bed. Then, switching on the night-light above her headboard, she pulled herself up and let her reeling senses guide her to the great bouquet of jasmine.

For a moment, she buried her face helplessly in their fragrance. Then, very tenderly, she broke a spray off to take to bed with her. There she cried herself to sleep, the sprig of yellow jasmine pressed between the pillow and her cheek.

Chapter Seven

*L*oralei awoke to an ugly dawn. The glory of yesterday's sunrise was a faded dream. In its place were long, bony fingers of gray which were neither darkness nor light. She did a quick bed check to make sure Amy had arrived safely last night. Finding her curled in a little fetal ball of rosy sleep, she groped her way to the shower before the pain of last night could come back to claw at her heart.

The floor of the cabin was tilted crazily so that she needed to hold onto the corner of the dressing table as she climbed the incline to the bathroom. It was hard to tell if the ship were moving or if the storm still raged. The atmosphere felt charged. And yet there was silence.

Gravity was misbehaving. But it was a relief to see that the bathroom lights shone as if all were quite correct. At least, at first they did. Then Loralei noted with a frown that little pink halos surrounded the bulbs on either side of the mirror.

She squeezed her eyes together for a moment then opened them experimentally. The halos were still there. Cold water. That would help. But, once her face was blotted dry with the soft towel, the halos had begun their unmistakable orbit of the bare bulbs. The beginnings of another headache. More frequent now. Just as the doctor had said they would be.

Trying not to disturb Amy, Loralei groped in the closet for a change of clothing. Fresh air. That would help. Fresh air and coffee. If only she could manage to get dressed—

But Amy had yawned herself awake, full of news as always.

"Where *were* you last night? You missed out on all the excitement! We had a 'Man Overboard' alert! Nobody knows for sure if he jumped or one of those waves—absolute *tidal* waves, Lory—washed him over the rail! It was ghastly—*ghastly!* Waves kept sucking him under—and once he was this close," Amy measured an arm's length, "trying to grab onto the brass curl of rail. Do you suppose he was sorry? I mean if he *jumped.*"

Even now, Amy's breath came in excited gasps. Loralei, whose heart had stopped completely, held onto the closet door for support. Unable to speak. Unable to breathe. *Jerrod!*

"Sometimes," Amy shuddered as she reached for her robe, "that treacherous ocean was as smooth as glass and he would try to fight to the surface and swim back, but the waves kept rolling—pushing him back—sucking him under! You could tell he was *choking*—"

"Amy—Amy—*please*—this man, did he get away—I mean, make it back?"

Amy stopped, took one look at Loralei, and sprang

from bed. In an instant, her hands had reached out to Loralei and eased her onto a small, upholstered chair.

"You look as if you're going to faint. You *are* ill! I knew it from the start—"

Loralei tore her friend's hands from her shoulders.

"Amy, tell me! I have to know!" The words were like shards against her throat, whispered because the sharp edges had cut into the flesh.

"The man couldn't have made it anywhere in that storm without help. A rescue team finally managed to get him in a lifeboat—but those of us who watched helped, too! Even the rescue team wouldn't have been able to pull this thing off without help from Up There. I prayed—we all did...Lory, you're shivering like we hit an iceberg instead of a tropical storm!"

Loralei tried to control the chattering of her teeth as she spoke.

"I'm thankful along with the rest of you," she managed to say.

"That's so like you—and you didn't even *see* the man! I'm going to lay out clothes for you."

Loralei nodded, her heart too full to speak.

Alive! Jerrod's alive! For in her mind there could be no question as to the "Man Overboard's" identity. And suddenly yesterday's problems receded into the past like some disappearing shoreline. The man she loved was safe and aboard ship. Nothing else mattered. Not even this explosive headache. Coffee would dull the ache. And seeing Jerrod would make her impervious to pain anyway.

Then there welled up within her heart a deep need to thank someone—the crew members and the Lord.

"My heart is on its knees," she whispered inside the

secret closet of her heart. The thought was aimed at nobody in particular, but immediately she felt better.

With a lift of spirit, Loralei looked at the off-the-shoulder cotton blouse Amy laid out, its soft yellows reminding her of shafts of today's missing sun, and the white wrap-around skirt. Obediently, she dressed. Then, almost happily, she lifted strand after strand of yellow coral necklaces and wound them around her neck. Swinging her hair up and securing it on top of her head, she added a tiny cluster of last night's jasmine.

She caught her breath when she surveyed the reflection. Her cheeks were flushed. Her eyes sparkled. Could the doctor be wrong? Doctors did mix medical records sometimes...but no, there could be no error. She had seen the X-rays, identical to her mother's. There was no chance...but she had this day!

There were few people in the dining room. All seasick, the head waiter whispered behind his hand. But it would pass. They would be heading into more placid waters. Yes, they had made a wide, sweeping turn and were heading back to Mazatlan.

Did the storm become a hurricane for real?

Oh, yes, she sure did, Lady Macbeth she was named! Vicious creature with winds up to 140 miles per hour had been expected to strike shore somewhere last night. Only she veered off, "woman-like" (the waiter looked at the two girls teasingly), and then blew herself out to sea.

Couldn't a hurricane change its mind?

Oh yes, not to be taken lightly, these hurricanes. That's why the captain thought it wise to take no chances. And 'twould be a fine trip—clearing no doubt—and beautiful in romantic Mazatlan.

Listening, Loralei let the dreams creep back into her heart. Stronger this time. The idea came slowly. Or did it? For once the thought surfaced, she realized that deep down inside her, it had been there all along. Just waiting for her to give it birth.

The waiter looked at her strangely when she all but sang out her order. "Chilled grapefruit—and, oh, papaya—*always* papaya! Muffins, coffee—and surprise me with the rest!"

She was ordering her wedding breakfast. Jerrod did not know it, but this was their wedding day. There was no waiting period in Mexico! She was through saying "No" to life, what little remained of it. Even if there were only a month, a week, *this day,* she wanted to spend it as Jerrod's wife. They would face his dilemma together as husband and wife—

With a start, Loralei realized that Amy was waving her hand in front of her.

"Yoo hoo! Remember me?"

"I'm sorry," Loralei murmured, but she knew that her eyes must be shining when she lifted them toward Amy for there appeared a puzzled look on the other girl's face.

"Now, you're the other Lory, my Sunshine Girl. You must have had a glimpse of Mystery Man! What gives with you two anyway?"

"I don't know what you're talking about," Loralei tried to pass it off lightly, but she felt the color rise to her face.

The waiter brought the chilled grapefruit, poured coffee, and disappeared. Loralei took a grateful sip of her coffee. Amber. Strong. Bracing. Her heart sang so loudly that surely Amy must hear it.

Mazatlan...Mazatlan...where if a honeymoon failed, the marriage didn't have a chance to begin with!

Her song was cut short by a voice. Familiar. Unmistakable. It wasn't real. Things like this just didn't happen...

"Loralei! Loralei!" Paul's golden body was striding toward her.

Paul...*he* was the stranded passenger...Paul...and before she could think further, she was caught in a bearhug.

"My word, Lory, *look!*" Amy's voice warned, her wide-eyed gaze fixed on the door. Loralei's heart turned over and stopped.

Jerrod!

Chapter Eight

*L*oralei only half-saw Paul. The Greek-god bronzeness of his body, the ripples of his muscles—more, it seemed, than most other men possessed—and the lightness of his voice were only vaguely familiar. Her fiance was a stranger, someone she had known in another life.

Her greeting, she thought later, must have been cold and unresponsive. Or did she make one at all? Her eyes as well as her heart were busy searching the room, the doors, and the corridors for the man she had known all her life—even before she met him.

But Jerrod was gone.

Loralei knew a sense of unreality. None of this was happening. And her headache was coming back. Through a mist of pain she sensed the presence of the ever-watchful waiter. He was greeting Paul warmly.

Would the gentleman like to join the lovely ladies for breakfast? Providing, of course—the waiter raised his eyebrows discretely as if seeking permission.

Speak, Loralei—speak! But her tongue remained frozen.

Amy saved the moment.

"Yes, indeed!" she said, using her usual anything-for-adventure voice. "As a matter of fact, the gentleman most likely will be joining us for the remainder of the cruise."

Amy then turned quickly to Loralei to explain.

"Poor Roz can't even digest the *word* when it comes to food! She'll be taking the first plane back home that she can squeeze into." Then, with a swing of her long, satin hair, she was looking back at Paul.

"And *you,*" she said, "have to be Lory's Golden Boy!"

"I'm sorry—" Loralei struggled to put words together, aware that her tongue was thick and that the faces in front of her swam, distorted, and merged. "Amy Farrell, Paul Teasdale."

Without feeling, Loralei saw Amy's dark-pooled eyes assessing the length and breadth of Paul. As objectively as one watches a movie, she realized that Paul was staring the way men always did when Amy was within sight.

How could they help it? She was everything both wholesome and mysterious in a woman. The white cotton casual she was wearing that morning emphasized her dark vivaciousness, adding a golden glow to her even suntan. So vibrant. So *alive!* Both of them. It was almost as if the warmth inside Amy were radiating to Paul... that the same blood coursed through their veins.

Giving Paul her full attention, Amy said, "Paul Teasdale—I recognized you from your pictures, only you're much more handsome in person. And you're trying out for the Olympics?"

Paul was dazzled, of course. He was used to having attractive girls swarm after him. Only not as beautiful as Amy—not as rich either.

But that was unfair thinking, Loralei realized in the only corner of her brain that seemed to be functioning. Paul had no way of knowing that Amy's father was *the* Everett Farrell, owner of countless oil fields operating throughout the world with offices as sprawled out as the state of Texas—

"Well, Loralei?"

Paul, having chatted with Amy for several moments, turned to face his fiancee—the moment she had dreaded. "Aren't *you* glad to see me?"

That one emphasized word said Paul would always be Paul. He attracted women like night-lights compelled moths—causing them to beat their wings to pieces in an effort to get inside the glass covering for even more light.

"You know I am," Loralei said truthfully. "It's just that I—well, I haven't recovered from the shock—"

He grinned.

"You should have known I would find you, that my curiosity would be aroused. And then when you wired me—"

"Oh, she understands, I'm sure," Amy said with a quick rush of words.

Color had risen to her cheeks and Loralei noted that the velvet eyes were averted so as not to meet her gaze. "But the weather—this storm—that's why she's shocked—that you could get through. Oh, but why," Amy affected a little pout, "should we talk about such mundane things as *weather?* It's going to be fun—now that you're here—huh, Lory?"

"Of course."

Loralei knew the words fell flat even though she tried to put welcome in her voice. This was wrong. All wrong. Every word was tightening the web of deception. *How, she wondered bitterly, could she have entertained the foolish notion that she could outrun her problems? She had only postponed facing them, compounding them, making them harder to solve—*

With a sudden jerk, she sat erect, startled by the idea that she was quoting the doctor. To her relief, she saw that the waiter had arrived with their orders. With trembling fingers, she picked up her fork.

Eat, even though food tasted like sawdust now. Make small talk, even though her throat ached with unshed tears. Listen to what Amy and Paul said...do *anything* that would ease the pain of facing reality.

But the jumbled thoughts came like monsters of the night. *I have a brain tumor...I am going to die...Jerrod (oh, Jerrod, I love you!), wonderful Jerrod is in deep trouble with what appears to be local, state, and federal officials.*

But none of this hurt really. They could have handled it—found a way...if only Amy had not sent for Paul...

Somehow she managed to say the appropriate things, at least respond when she was spoken to, but when Amy engaged Paul in conversation about medals won and hoped for, Loralei leaned back exhausted.

If she could just rest a moment —

That's when another beautiful fantasy came to mind.

At first, she and Jerrod were in a crowd that trudged along the Malecon, the great seawall embankment separating Mazatlan from the beaches along the Pacific. The tropical sun was without mercy. It was hard to breathe. Then, mercifully, the sun tucked its hot chin behind the palm trees. The crowds surged toward the city, giving frenzied cries, "Coco loco...dining...dancing...eat, drink, and be merry—for tomorrow you die!"

"Open your eyes, my darling, they're gone," Jerrod was whispering against her ear. And everything was wonderful. The crowds and their hateful words were forgotten. Trade winds cooled her burning cheeks. The western sky shot tongues of orange flame across the blue arch of the sky, picking up the liquid silver of Jerrod's eyes. For a beautiful moment, she drowned in their love-lit depths, and then her strength returned.

They were running, she and Jerrod—running past the hotel where the "Mexican Fiesta Night" put a whirl of color like an escaped rainbow throughout the rooms and down onto the narrow streets...past the curio shops, boys diving for exotic shells, and bullfighting posters... waving away grinning hack drivers to head for the path they both knew so well.

"You brought the ring?" she whispered breathlessly as they paused on the steep incline.

Jerrod's answer was a kiss, then another, and another. He was crushing her bouquet of jasmine against her clothes, bruising the beautiful yellow flowers so that their aroma was even more intoxicating.

It didn't matter...it didn't matter...their world was filled with wild jasmine from which she could pick a little sprig at any given moment...they hugged her heart and the church ahead...

"Loralei—*Loralei!*"

A dreamy, little smile began somewhere inside. Then stopped. For it was Amy who called her name and there was alarm in her voice...whisking Jerrod away...erasing the fantasy...

"Lory, are you all right?" This time it was Paul. "But, of course, you aren't!" he answered his own question.

She must protest, tell him she was all right. Make him believe it. It was a part of the game. But Paul had turned to Amy to explain.

"She's been under a doctor's care. Only," he defended himself, "I didn't know—so busy with my practice and all that goes with it. I didn't know, that is, until the doctor began calling her roommate, looking for Lory—"

"Paul!"

Loralei heard the edge in her own voice. She had no idea how much he knew, but she wanted to stop this. Amy mustn't know. Or Jerrod. Most of all, Jerrod. *If* she ever saw Jerrod again—after he had seen her in the arms of another man...

Chapter Nine

*W*aves, still high, had lost some of their fury. Swells rocked the ship but with less anger. The sky was still sullen, but the rain had stopped. Only the wind refused to let the storm die. Tormented, it whipped at the flags and pushed against any passengers who ventured out on the slippery decks.

"We'll be able to talk out there," Paul said, pushing against the door leading to the wind-whipped deck.

Loralei shook her head.

"We couldn't stand up in that wind, Paul—let alone hope to hear each other. Besides," she insisted when he continued to shove at the heavy door, "you're not used to the sun's rays—"

"Sun! Old Sol hasn't shown his face for days!"

Ignoring her warning, Paul went on with pushing against the force of the wind—determined, as always, to beat down resistance. The door yielded just as Loralei spoke and she doubted that he heard her words.

"The sun doesn't have to shine for you to burn here so near to the Tropic of Cancer—Paul!"

But he had stepped outside. Now he held the door open and motioned for her to follow. Loralei wished for her umbrella from Mazatlan. Not that she could hold it in this wind. But she did not want to let go of the beautiful memory it held...

For a moment, as she took Paul's hand and tried to get her balance on deck, Loralei let herself remember the day, the one perfect day, that she and Jerrod had shared. In it they had grown to know each other better, to understand, and to love one another more than some people managed in a lifetime.

She would cherish it forever no matter what her *forever* held. But for now she must deal with the present. See what she could shape from the hopeless clay that her life had become.

"Your friend's got a lot of class..." Amy, Loralei was sure Paul meant, but the wind sucked the rest of his words away. This was no good. She would never be able to hear his voice. And yet he went on speaking. "—and tactful of her—need to be alone—"

Loralei nodded, being reasonably sure what Paul meant. But there was no need in trying to answer. The wind was whipping her hair into her face without mercy. Her eyes stung and her throat felt dry. And what on earth was Paul saying?

"Why, Lory, *why?*" she made out. Then the rest was a hopeless jumble. "—everything going for us—no explanation—won't give up—shouldn't have left training—whole future—but the doctor said emergency—"

"I can't hear you, Paul!" Loralei cried out. But she knew Paul did not hear that either. Instead of listening, he was reaching into his sweater pocket, removing a sealed envelope and handing it to her.

Pushing the hair from her eyes, Loralei tried to take the envelope. But there was a fierce gust of wind. She staggered against its force, was thrown against the door, and the envelope was picked up like a wisp of thistledown and blown over the rail.

For one horrified moment, she watched it bob gracefully up and down like a gull on the smaller waves. Then there was a sudden wall of water which cut into her face with stinging salt spray. And the letter was gone. Unopened. Unread. Out into the open sea.

Sobered, Paul helped her back inside and pulled out a chair from one of the little semi-private tables for two.

"I'm sorry, Loralei. I really am." *He was sorry*.

"What was it, Paul?" she asked through stiff lips, knowing that his answer would be important.

"My reason for being here," he said sheepishly, then embarrassed at what he had said, Paul added, "I mean—the letter *and* your invitation. That helped, believe me!"

"Paul, I didn't—" But Loralei stopped there. This was not the time. She must deal with the letter first. Then somehow she must find a way to tell him why she couldn't marry him—well, one of the reasons. There were two now. She would have to tell him about Jerrod...only there wasn't anything really to tell...

"What was it, Paul?" she repeated. "The letter—who wrote it—what was in it—"

"It came from Dr. Morse. He kept calling—first your roommate, then me. You put us at a disadvantage, you know?"

"I know. I wish there had been another way."

Paul wiped a drop of water from his nose with a wet

handkerchief. "We began thinking we would be accused of doing away with your body—"

Loralei felt the nerves along her spine tighten. *Already they were all speaking of her as if she were a corpse,* she thought a little wildly. Then, with determination, she put aside such notions.

"What did Dr. Morse want?" she asked, fearing his answer.

Paul's laugh filled the room.

"Want? How would I know? Doctors don't talk. They just write in their little black books. I remember when I strained a leg muscle—but that was critical at the time, being so soon before the Olympics."

A strained leg muscle was important. . . an inoperable brain tumor obviously was not . . .

"Did he tell you anything, Paul?"

He shook his head and then leaned toward her, concern showing on the planes of his handsome face.

"Say, this is not something serious, is it, Lory? Obviously, there's something you haven't told me?" Paul shook his tawny head as if trying to absorb a totally new idea. "You mean the letter had something to do with your leaving—and it's what that man knows that's keeping us apart?"

Here it was. The moment of truth. But Loralei suddenly found that she did not know how to handle it. Once that would have been her reason. Her only reason. Now she knew it wasn't that simple. Now she knew what love, *real* love, was. Now there was Jerrod.

"Lory!"

There was an edge to Paul's voice. He did not like to be kept waiting. Everything was time-clocked. *Maybe,* she thought—feeling a little sorry for Paul—*if I told him*

*the diagnosis, he would need to know the exact date of
my demise.*

"Yes—yes, and no, Paul."

"That's no answer at all!"

"It's all I can give you right now. Try to be patient—
I'll tell you what!" Loralei forced a note of brightness.
"You're here—"

"Thanks to my trainer who thought I needed a rest!"
Paul leaned back comfortably. He always was more at
ease talking about himself than about others.

"And I agree with him. You've pushed hard. So why
not make the most of whatever time you have—"

"I'm flying home from Mazatlan. But that gives a day
and a night."

Loralei inhaled deeply, knowing that Paul would never
understand the meaning of her next words.

"A lot can happen to change our lives in that time,"
she said softly.

"You drive a hard bargain!" But there was a grin on
his face. "O.K. All aboard. Away from the cares of
yesterday. Away from our land-locked routine. And into a lighthearted world."

"Remember you're in training," Loralei tried to maintain the upbeat mood. "And now let's get into some dry
clothes."

Paul pulled his long, golden frame from the chair. "I'm
for that. Then you'll show me around—or do you need
to rest? You look beat. But Amy is a very good guide,
I'm sure."

Amy, they found, was only too happy to take Paul on
a tour of the ship. But was Loralei sure she felt like being alone? Loralei assured the two of them over and over
that being alone was exactly what she did need. Later they

would plan their evening. . . Amy and Paul were at the
door. . . soon solitude would be hers. . . oh, blessed
thought! But at the door Amy paused. Turning back to
Loralei, she half-whispered something about a note so
that Paul, who had stepped into the hall, would not hear.
With a bob of her head toward the dressing table, Amy
was gone.

With more strength than she knew she had remaining,
Loralei ran to pick up a small envelope with her name
scrawled across it, undoubtedly delivered by the steward.
With trembling fingers, she ripped open the flap. *Oh,
please—please—let it be from him—oh, please—*

It was! "Can you meet me in the usual place at 4:00?
J"

The usual place. That would be the dining room. It
would be deserted between lunch and dinner. Jerrod was
meeting her there. They would be together. The whole
world lighted up with the hidden sun. Everything was
beautiful, wonderful. Fatigue was gone and her headache
didn't matter!

Loralei tried to rest but found it was impossible. She
brushed her hair until it gave off burnished lights, filed
her nails, and looked through the blouses and skirts Amy
had sorted out for her use.

Dreamily, she held up a candy-pink striped silk sports
dress. Casual. Cool. Its understated elegance lending
color to her pale face. Now that the storm was subsiding,
surely the pallor would go away. And the halos around
the lights and people's faces would fade. *Everything*
would be right once she was with Jerrod. Yes, she would
wear the pink.

With an eye on her watch, Loralei munched on an apple from the nightly basket of fruit the steward had

delivered. That would be lunch, dinner—oh, surely they could find a way to spend the evening together!

Fifteen minutes before four, Loralei slipped into the deserted dining room and made her way to the little alcove. Allowing anticipation to fill her being with joy, she looked out the porthole to watch the restless sea. No calm had come to the waters yet, but the high-cresting waves were beautiful to watch.

Were they, she wondered, more beautiful than those in Santa Monica? Or was she more tuned in to everything lovely these days because she was in love—made more picture-perfect because her heart knew that their world couldn't last?

Four o'clock! When there was the muffled sound of footsteps, Loralei's heart started its familiar pounding. She would rush into his arms...no, she would close her eyes in the little game they played...and Jerrod would claim a kiss...

When there was no further sound, Loralei opened her eyes. Nobody stood near. The room had grown darker and shadows seemed to lurk in the corners. There was no sound except for the wash of the waves. Some instinct, however, warned her of danger.

Apprehensive, she half-rose from the table. And then she sat down quickly and slunk deep into the upholstered chair. The man she saw was Max Avery!

Maybe, if she could be very still, the F.B.I. agent would not see her and she could make a getaway. When at last the man turned away as if trying to watch both the elevators and stairs, Loralei bent low and half-crawled between the tables until she was able to slip out through the doors as she and Jerrod had done only the evening before.

With a wildly-beating heart, Loralei hurried to the stairs, not daring to wait for the elevator. When curious eyes looked her way, she purposely slowed her steps and walked with as much dignity as possible up the first flight. At the landing she was tempted to run. And then she slowed her steps, aware that she was being followed.

Risking a casual glance over her shoulder was costly. The stairs seemed to rise and crest like the waves as a sudden wash of dizziness overcame her.

Maybe the shock of what she saw...maybe the "prognosis" the doctor had given. Whatever the cause, Loralei knew that escape was impossible now. The man immediately behind her was Captain Max Avery and he was laying a restraining hand on her shoulder.

In paralyzed awe, she allowed herself to be gently but firmly moved aside so that the other guests could pass by them.

"You wished to see me?" Loralei forced her voice to remain calm.

"I *must* ask your cooperation, Miss Coleman." The man's face was expressionless and his low voice told her nothing.

Loralei pulled away, hoping that her trembling legs would support her. "I do not know this man—Theron Somebody."

"Stone," he said. "I cannot impress upon you enough the importance of our finding him. Otherwise—" he looked at her significantly, "we might arrest the wrong man!"

"What's he done—this Theron Stone? And what makes you persist in linking me with a man whom I have never met?"

"If I gave the impression that I was linking you with

him, I apologize," he said curtly. "However, indications are that you might be in a position to help. And, as to what he has done, I can only say that he is in deep trouble as my presence here should indicate."

"Money? Has he taken money?" Loralei's words were a whisper.

Avery's eyes sharpened. "How did you know that?"

Loralei tried to affect a careless tone of voice.

"I didn't," she shrugged. "Love of money just seems to be the root of all evil, doesn't it, Captain? And now, if I am free to go?"

Max Avery stepped aside.

"Of course." But his eyes told her that he would be watching.

Even after the man disappeared down the bend of the stairs, Loralei stood pressed against the wall, too shaken to move.

I'm overtaxing myself, she thought dully, *maybe to the point where I can't get back home.* A great yearning to see Jerrod washed over her.

Then, blessedly, he was there. Gathering her in his strong arms. Pulling her head against his chest where, even through the tweedy scratch of the sport coat he wore, Loralei could feel the heavy pounding of his heart. He held her close—so close she was unable to breathe—and the yearning inside her eased.

"It's a miracle," she whispered. "A miracle that you are always here when I need you."

"It's a miracle our being together at all. And the greatest miracle of all is that I need *you,* my darling, as much—no, *more* than!—you need me!"

Oblivious to the passing onlookers, they embraced on the stairs, their bodies melting into one. With the love

inside her so overpowering that it could no longer be
denied, Loralei realized then that nothing must keep them
apart.

Nothing! What was it Solomon's Song said? "...love
is as strong as death...Many waters cannot quench love;
neither can the floods drown it..."

Jerrod was whispering in her ear, "—so hold my hand.
The little chapel is almost always empty—"

And, not caring where they went, Loralei allowed
herself to be guided down two flights of stairs and into
a small room, the semi-darkness mellowed by candlelight
flickering on the faces of sculptured statues. Jerrod felt
his way between a pew and kneeling bench in the darkest
corner, sat down, and pulled her gently down beside him.

"There's not a moment to waste," he whispered.

She nodded. There never is. She wished fervently that
the world was aware of what she and Jerrod had discovered.

"At first, I thought I could protect you—hold back
the truth."

There was a little groan in the whispered words and,
even in the darkness, Loralei could see the muscles in Jerrod's face tighten with emotion.

"Fool that I was," he went on, "I even promised
myself that I would ask nothing of you—"

"Ask anything, Jerrod. I will do anything. Just name
it!"

When he was silent, Loralei prompted an answer.
"What do you want of me, darling?"

"The truth, Lory."

The little cry was out before Loralei could stop it. And
then she relaxed, almost laughing hysterically in her relief.
Paul! Jerrod wanted to know about Paul.

"You mean about the man—the one who boarded in Cabo San Lucas? I can explain—"

But Jerrod interrupted the little half-truth she was planning. "About him, yes. But there is more. We've both behaved foolishly—kept secrets from each other. I can't ask you to share my life—such as I have or will have—until I share what I am. What I really am."

Almost fiercely, she snatched both his hands, folded them together and pulled them against her glowing cheeks.

"It doesn't matter! I don't care—"

Gently, Jerrod withdrew one hand to place it lightly against her lips.

"It matters to me, Loralei. I have to be true to myself and to God. Otherwise, I could not love you as I do!"

The moment was too fragile to spoil with words. Loralei could only close her eyes in the little chapel and let the beauty of the words penetrate her lids, enter the capillaries of her being leading to the heart and the very soul. For suddenly she knew again that it would outlast the body. A love like this began on earth. But it didn't—it *couldn't*—end there.

Solomon was right. Love was the conqueror. It could not be destroyed by fire, quenched by water. Even death had no power over it—or, she realized with a start, over *her!*

"I understand," was all she could manage.

Then, checking the doors again, Jerrod made sure there was no audience before telling her the incredible story. Later, she supposed it would make more sense. For now she could only listen. Not respond. She and Jerrod would be reunited somewhere, somehow, just as she had been reunited suddenly with God who had waited so patiently in the wings until she acknowledged His presence again...

Jerrod had been poor, very poor, in his childhood, a childhood cut short by the death of his father. But his mother was determined that he have an education even though the sacrifice was that she must work long hours in a garment factory. Only later did he realize that she had been ill all the while.

Jerrod's voice quivered and broke. Loralei brought his head to her face, and, leaning to kiss him, felt the tears coursing down his cheeks as they coursed down her own. But he must go on. It was important to them. So, forcing herself to push her head away, Loralei whispered, "Yes, Jerrod?"

He had graduated and landed his first job by the time full knowledge of her condition was revealed. And with it the news of a new kind of surgery, experimental and unpromising as yet, providing one was willing to stand the expenses insurance companies were unwilling to underwrite.

Jerrod's breathing quickened, causing his words to rush out. He was little more than errand boy for World Wide Computers, a much smaller company then. There, he had formed a friendship with his employer's son—a friendship which proved invaluable when he learned the gravity of his mother's condition. No money. Banks would not lend.

And so you "borrowed" from the company, Jerrod?

Yes, but conscience dictated that he confide in the friend. The surgery was unsuccessful. He was five thousand dollars in debt. But Theron covered for him—

"Theron! Theron *Stone?*"

"Theron Stone." His whisper echoed against the walls

of the empty room. The friend who stood by. Trusted him. Protected him. The friend to whom he owed everything.

"So what have you done for him, Jerrod?"

The words were wrenched from Loralei. The whole picture was agonizingly clear even before Jerrod answered her.

"What I had to do." Jerrod swept an impatient hand at the stubborn wave which dipped down onto his forehead. "What any loyal friend would do—"

"Oh, no! You didn't. You couldn't have—*stolen* for him!"

"No—no, I didn't do that. In fact, I would have tried to talk him out of it—but that is beside the point. I wish before God I hadn't been the one who found the discrepancy—my friend, who helped me to where I am today."

Oh, Jerrod, it's because of him you ARE where you are today! Can't you see he was setting you up?

And then the idea came. Amy! Amy would help. Since Jerrod had taken the blame for the missing funds, Amy could help. Maybe this was the "cause" Amy needed.

"How much, Jerrod? How much did Theron Stone take?"

"Five million."

"Dollars! Five million *dollars!*"

A wild laugh rose to her lips, a laugh without mirth. She wasn't even sure how many zeros there were in such a staggering sum!

Then suddenly Loralei sat bolt upright.

"But wait! These men who have been following me, asking questions—they must not believe *you* took the money. Otherwise, they would be looking for *you.*"

"They expect he can lead them to me, I think. Oddly
enough, the two of us look very much alike and the in-
vestigators are strangers to us both. Oh, they'll find me.
I've accepted that. They were just a jump behind in checking the locker—"

"Mine?"

Even before he nodded, Loralei was putting the picture together with more clarity now. Of course. And
that's how they knew her name. But one thing still puzzled her.

"Who is the man with the strange eyes, the older
man?"

Jerrod admitted he didn't know. Then, inhaling
deeply, he said, "Well, there it is. And now my plans.
I have decided that I have to turn myself in, Loralei. I
guess I knew all along I couldn't go through with this.
But meeting you made me see more clearly. I had planned
to try for a contact in Cabo San Lucas. Now, it'll have
to be in Mazatlan—if I can just avoid arrest by Avery
or one of the less obvious agents—"

When he paused, Loralei tensed. Was someone at the
door?

But Jerrod's words were, "Oh, Lory, do you know
how you make a man feel? That alert, interested expression you wear as if you were clinging to my every
word—"

I am, Jerrod! I am, my darling! Her heart was crying
even as he went on talking, almost to himself.

"I don't like myself for what I'm about to do. But then
I don't like what I'll have to live with if I don't. That's
the problem with deception.

"There comes a time when we realize that a half-truth
is a half-lie. Our God of Love is also the God of Truth.

Now," Jerrod drew a deep breath, "do you still love me?"

"More than ever!" Loralei whispered with a rush of emotion. "If that were possible. And I'll stick by whatever decision you reach—"

Loralei felt her voice weaken. What could she promise him really? All the tensions of the day piled up, causing a queasiness within her. The heavy, warm air of the chapel enclosed her and the jerking motion of the ship became unpleasant. She leaned toward Jerrod who immediately seemed to sense her need and laid a protective arm across her shoulders. She felt the tears come then— first to fill her near-green eyes, then to spill down her cheeks and soak through the candy-striped silk of her dress.

"What will they do to you, Jerrod? You didn't take the five million dollars. Surely, you aren't going to insist that you did."

Jerrod held her close against him.

"No," he whispered in her hair. "I've thought about it and I guess the best thing's to let the authorities take the lead. But let's not build false hopes. My withdrawal of the confession I left behind will lead to a line of questioning that will cause me to betray Theron—"

"But you'll be cleared."

"Hardly. Most likely, it'll come out that I dipped into the funds myself at one time. They may not find me too credible a witness—and certainly not a desirable employee. I don't know what kind of life I can offer you—or when—oh, Lory," a little groan escaped him, "what am I doing? We've spent all the time we can hope for on me when it's you we must talk about. This man— who is he—*what* is he in your life?"

Loralei gave up trying to find the right words.

"He, Paul, is a friend—how else can I put it? He has a brilliant career ahead and his tawny good looks would capture the heart of any girl. He has a dream, Jerrod. Not like your bells—a dream of cheering audiences while he accepts a gold medal—as he will, I'm sure. But Paul—Paul's a boy who never became a man."

"Where does he fit into your life?" Jerrod's whisper was almost inaudible.

Loralei turned to him with a little open-mouth gasp she was unable to explain.

"Nowhere! Nowhere at all, Jerrod—now that I've met you. Maybe not even before. Right now I can't seem to remember whose idea marriage was—"

When she paused, he whispered, "Go ahead, my darling, I will understand."

Oh, blessed Jerrod. No harsh words. No recriminations for her vague answer when he had asked regarding another man in her life. Just supporting her now. Understanding.

"I sent him a note when I left on this sudden trip. It was so cowardly—"

Jerrod's little chuckle broke the tension.

"As my grandmother would say, 'The kettle should not call the pot black!' "

"What you did was different," Loralei defended. "And to be fair, maybe I would have behaved differently except that I was still in shock—"

The truth, Loralei. You have to tell Jerrod the truth. The God of Love is the God of Truth.

"Oh, Jerrod, Jerrod! I wish you had met another girl—" Loralei whispered with a dry sob catching in her aching throat.

Jerrod leaned forward, encircled her in his arms, and drew her head onto his shoulder.

"If I had met another girl, I would still be looking for *you,* my darling. Whatever it is, tell me. We will share it as we are sharing this terrible blight in my own life."

From the warm circle of Jerrod's arms, Loralei watched in fascination as one of the candles at the altar fluttered and gasped for breath. Then, having melted to the end of its wick, it went out—leaving the world around them a little darker.

"I'm going to die, Jerrod."

The strong arms around her tightened. An embrace she would always remember in her short life forever. Its warmth was still with her when the spotlight flashed to illuminate their hiding place.

Chapter Ten

*L*ater Loralei would try to assemble the succeeding events so that they made some kind of sense. Right now, it was impossible. The blinding light...the sight of a helmeted head, faceless, it seemed...the sudden surge forward of the figure in the doorway—toward *her!* Seeming purposely to brush against her left shoulder as if causing her to lose her balance were the object...it was all a horror film, spinning forward from one reel to another ...not intended for the human eye to focus on any one picture long enough to grasp the plot...

Through a white haze of shock and fear, Loralei heard the muffled sounds of two men wrestling—the unknown assailant and Jerrod. Echoes of the men's movements seemed to bounce against the walls of the chapel to mingle with her half-stifled scream as she saw the stranger—he was wearing a yellow slicker, she realized—flick open a switchblade.

"Jerrod! Look out! He has a knife!"

This time her voice was a scream.

"Drop it." Jerrod's voice was low and controlled.

There was a soft thud. And then the strange figure was gone. How could he have escaped? Or maybe he had dropped to the floor to lie in hiding.

She tried to still the wild beating of her heart and listen. But the only sounds she could hear came from the outside—unhappy sounds of people who had too much leisure, too much food and drink, too much of everything.

"Stand very still," Jerrod whispered into her ear. Then he flattened himself against the wall and moved like a shadow to stand at the doorway.

Seconds stretched out while she stood motionless, listening as she knew Jerrod was, for some sound. When there was none, he motioned to her.

"Run for it, darling," he whispered when she was by his side.

"I can't leave you—" Loralei's words were a plea.

"Go, *please!*" Jerrod's words were desperate. "Get to your cabin. I'll contact you—"

And with that he parted the velvet drapes and pushed her gently into the corridor. Loralei was never to remember whether she ran up the stairs or down—or maybe she took the elevator. There seemed to be no time between Jerrod's gentle push and her fumbling with the key to her cabin.

There was trouble with the lock. Her hands trembled. Her head throbbed. And there was a stab of pain in her left shoulder. The man must have hit her harder than she realized.

When at last the key protestingly fit into the lock, the door swung open. And what she saw was as great a shock as any of the other string of events of this strange and frightening day.

Paul sat straddling the chair of her dressing table. A strand of sun-bleached hair fell appealingly over his forehead, but there was a familiar scowl on his boyish face.

Again, Loralei had the feeling that her former fiancé was a stranger. Familiar only in the way all national monuments are familiar. Actors. Newscasters. Olympic stars. Perfect, clean, and beautiful when viewed in pictures. But Paul now seemed bland and meaningless.

Loralei was unaware that he had risen until she was in his arms. In his arms and yet his voice was cross.

"I looked everywhere for you. You were supposed to stay put. Remember? Amy was worried."

Amy was worried. But what about you, Paul?

Lightly, hoping not to make a scene, Loralei disengaged herself.

"I'm sorry, Paul. Something came up. I—I was called away."

He pushed impatiently at the hair on his forehead.

"It was—well, a little embarrassing to say the least, seeing that I came all this way to be with you. At *your* invitation!"

Loralei opened her mouth and then closed it. There had been a look of pleading in Amy's face when the matter came up before.

Let Paul think what he wished. It didn't matter. It didn't matter at all. What really mattered was Jerrod's safety! She must get Paul out of the room in case Jerrod tried to contact her.

"I'm very tired, Paul."

The words she spoke were the truth. It had been such

a trying day and there was still a stab of pain in her arm. She winced as she pulled the shoulder strap of her bag from her arm.

But Paul was not to be rushed. He only rushed others.

"Not so fast! After all, there are matters that need to be set straight. I'll be leaving Mazatlan tomorrow night and I'm not leaving without some answers. You've been behaving strangely—particularly for a girl who's engaged."

Loralei raised a hand to rub her aching arm, but Paul reached out to grab it.

"Well, Lory!"

"We aren't engaged, Paul—not any more. I left you the note."

"Followed by a cablegram to join you. What in heaven's name is wrong with you? Here I was prepared for a needed vacation and some romancing—and I end up working out. Say," and there was a sudden upsweep in his voice, "that Amy is no slouch when it comes to leg work! Joined me in everything I did today—you've seen the gym?"

Loralei shook her head and Paul finished with a note of admiration, "I believe that girl would have donned gloves and gone a round or two of boxing with me if I would have allowed it."

Loralei felt a rush of gratitude mixed with envy. It was typical of Amy to step in where men were concerned, but she had filled a real need today. So the ache of envy she felt was not for the other girl's ravishing beauty but the vitality within her body. Vitality Loralei herself no longer felt.

"I wish I had been able to do that," she said, meaning it. "But as to the engagement, Paul, there isn't any.

There never should have been. We're not right for each other.''

Paul looked perplexed. And his words, when they came, seemed to be for himself maybe even more than for her.

"Then how come we're engaged?"

"I don't know," Loralei said honestly. "I just don't know—unless you found me a little different—'stand-offish,' you used to call it. Maybe that was a challenge?"

When he frowned, she was sure she had come very close to the truth. Paul always saw himself as the irresistible force for which there was no immovable object. One simply vaulted it with a high jump if a technical knockout wouldn't win the trophy.

"But you, Loralei—you never seemed that unwilling once I broke down that reserve!"

"I wasn't unwilling at all," she admitted. "You are in many ways what every young girl dreams of, you know. I was flattered—"

"Then what the heck! I don't get it. I don't get it at all. Tell you what. Let's forget the wedding thing, pretend we're just meeting, and maybe we'll fall in love again—"

A new love. Another challenge.

But she was too weary to argue or explain. What did it matter anyway? What did anything matter unless she could be with Jerrod? Oh, where was he?

Suddenly, crazily, Paul had two pairs of eyes. Then two faces. Followed by a dozen faces that floated before her eyes. To steady herself, Loralei reached out with her right arm, aware of the burning in her left one.

Paul, noticing nothing except her outstretched hand, took the gesture as one of consent.

"Good," he said, springing forward to embrace her lightly.

And then he gasped. "What on earth!" Paul looked at his hands.

Dully, she saw the bloodstains on his white cotton shirt. Paul noticed them, too, and drew back. As he released her, Loralei's eyes traveled to her left hand and saw that blood was welling steadily into it from a jagged slash just beneath the fabric of her dress on the left shoulder.

The helmeted stranger...the knife...she had been wounded! The many faces of Paul closed in around her as weakly she sank to the floor.

★   ★   ★

The ceiling above her was white, Loralei knew without opening her eyes. So the man feeling her pulse would be wearing a white coat. And there was no mistaking the smell of antiseptic. She had fallen. That was it. She had fallen and injured her head. That accounted for the awful ache.

The doctor was speaking. To her? Or was there someone else in the room?

"How did it happen—the knife wound?"

Paul was floundering for words, making everything he said sound like a denial of guilt.

Didn't he know doctors were non-judgmental—like Christians ought to be? But Paul didn't know much about Christians...just what she had told him...and lately she had been a poor example, losing her own faith for a time. Yet trying to uphold others in theirs. What was she anyway, the Lord's left hand?

The thought seemed to make more sense than the voices around her, so she let them fade away.

When they penetrated the inner layer of her consciousness again, Loralei was able to make out the doctor's words.

"It's a clean wound. Good that you brought her in. No need to transfuse her. But there's something else—"

When the man paused, Paul seemed interested.

"You mean—you mean, Loralei has something else wrong?"

"Are you her husband?"

"You mean she's *pregnant!* Could that be what—"

The doctor's voice was sharp then.

"I said no such thing! And I only meant that I am unable to discuss the patient's existing condition with an outsider. I will talk with Miss Coleman when she's awake. And for now she needs rest. May I suggest that you leave her with me for at least the next hour?"

Paul made no protest. Moments later she heard the door swish partly closed behind him.

"You can open your eyes now. He's gone!"

Loralei had the sudden, wild desire to laugh. How childish of her to think she was fooling the man. A doctor could tell by the pulse one's degree of consciousness.

But the lined face wth the beaked nose, down which the heavy-lensed glasses had slipped, did not look amused. Neither was there amusement in his voice.

"How long has it been since you saw a doctor?"

Loralei tried to sit up only to be pushed back onto the examining table firmly. "Last week," she said meekly.

"You're from Santa Monica your—er—"

"Friend," Loralei supplied. "Paul Teasdale."

"—Mr. Teasdale tells me. There's a specialist there I want you to see—a neurologist. I'm going to be in touch with him and suggest a series of tests."

"No—no, please don't bother, doctor. You see, I know about the tumor already. That *is* what you're talking about?" Loralei asked, realizing that for the first time she had spoken the word aloud and with as much objectivity as one speaks of weather.

The man looked surprised.

"Yes. Yes, it is. And the sooner we get at the thing—"

"It's inoperable," she told him. "I've seen the X-rays—and accepted death as inevitable. My mother had the same—"

The door burst all the way open.

Jerrod—blessed Jerrod—rushed toward her to sweep her into his arms in a way that told her he had already heard.

Chapter Eleven

*W*hen Loralei promised to rest the required hour, the doctor walked from his office, murmuring something about checking on some of the passengers in their rooms. Alone, she and Jerrod embraced and shared a long, deep kiss. Then, lying in the protective circle of his arms, she listened to the short finish of the incredible incident that had happened in the chapel.

"I found the knife," Jerrod said, "but I am mystified by the disappearance of the man—whoever he was. Did you get a glimpse of his face?"

Loralei hadn't. Neither had Jerrod. So there was little to go on. Except "Exhibit A," the weapon. Shouldn't he turn it in to the captain or somebody and alert him that there was a possible murderer aboard?

No, Jerrod decided, not until he could contact the proper authorities, give himself up, be assured of protection until he could reach the States.

What could be the motive for such an attack? he

wondered. Loralei was no help. The assailant certainly was not aligned with Captain Max Avery and somehow she didn't think he had any connection with the older man with the pompadour.

When there was a pause, Loralei snuggled a little closer to Jerrod. She felt stronger now and there was a sense of reality.

"I saw Paul."

"Did you tell him about us?"

"No—there wasn't time. But I made him see that we weren't right for each other."

Jerrod pushed the tendrils of hair from her forehead and brushed her brow with a kiss.

"You mean he agreed to give you up just like that? What kind of a man can he be? Don't ask that of *me*, Lory," he whispered huskily.

"I wouldn't—I mean, I won't—not the same way. But—you heard, didn't you?"

"I won't pretend that I didn't." Jerrod pressed his cheek to her brow. "But, darling," his voice was tender, "we all must die. It is the sad-sweet story of our mortality. Only that way can our immortality begin!"

Oh, Jerrod, Jerrod! Only you could say a thing like that. But she could not trust her voice to express those thoughts verbally.

It was Jerrod who spoke again. Gently. Softly.

"It may seem strange to you right now that you are centered out to look behind the curtain of your mortality. Maybe you're luckier than the rest of us.

"Already, you have observed new glory in each sunrise, discovered the beauty of a tropical storm, and realized the fragility of every living moment. What's more, you have allowed me to see it with you. And that is why we must be together come what may. Are you listening, darling?"

She nodded through a silvery mist of tears—born more of joy than sadness. This moment meant more to her than all tomorrows.

"Very simply, yes or no. Will you marry me, Lory?"

"But how—you must—I have this—" And then she burst into a flood of tears. "Oh, yes, yes, Jerrod— *yes!*"

Jerrod held her so closely that Loralei was uncertain whether it was his heart or hers that pounded in her ears to all but drown out his words. Both, she was sure—and in perfect syncopation. His words were like a song in her ear.

"If I thought it possible, I would say the little church in Mazatlan—remember?" Of course, she remembered, Loralei's nod said. "But after we go ashore—I can't promise—"

"I know, darling. I know."

"But the captain performs the ceremonies, you know. I've already spoken with him—"

"Oh, but there has to be jasmine—wild jasmine!"

Such a whimsical little detail in the face of all else. But so important. "And bells—some kind of bells!" Their ringing would symbolize the continuation of Jerrod's dream.

"Just one word about our future—and then we will bury it the way some people do the past! I don't know what the outcome will be for me—how much time we can have—afterward."

Oh, Jerrod, her heart cried out, *there may not be any future!*

"But you must promise me one thing, Lory."

"Anything—*anything!*"

"I want you to do as the doctor says."

"It will do no good—just raise false hopes—I can live with death now."

"One doesn't live with *death*. One lives with life. That takes courage. Give me your promise, Lory."

"Not that," she sobbed. "I went through it with Mother—"

He was silent for what seemed a long time. When he spoke it was a different Jerrod than she had known before. Powerful. Commanding. Persuasive. And *wonderful!*

"We've had a problem, Lory, you and I—until now. We have been guilty of trying to resolve our problems without Supreme help. We have no right to do that. Faith means turning these things over to God. Are you willing to do that?"

"I am willing," she said softly.

Peace came then. Real peace. The kind she knew Jerrod was experiencing as she saw his lips move in silent prayer.

Tonight she, too, would pray, pouring out the words she had held imprisoned in her heart for so long. But for now she could only lie motionless watching Jerrod's wonderful face in adoration. An adoration that went so deep within her soul that it became a prayer within itself—a prayer of praise to the God of Love and Truth who had sent her this man to serve as His mouthpiece . . .

When at length Jerrod's lips were still, he lifted his head to look deeply into her eyes. There was a gleam of triumph in his once-haunted eyes, but his words were realistic.

"It won't be easy, any of it, little Lory. Look what has happened to you already—and because of me."

There was pain in his voice which hurt Loralei more deeply than the flesh wound she had sustained in the chapel.

"It's nothing. Doesn't even hurt anymore since it's been bandaged. And we can praise the Lord together that He has bound up our hearts—"

A polite knock on the door interrupted her words. The doctor entered, nodded, and walked to where Loralei lay.

Jerrod rose as the professional man peered into her eyes with a light, appeared about to say something more, and then put his hand to her elbow to help her from the examination table.

"Well, you may return to your cabin. We need your bed!" he said brusquely. Then, even as Loralei was about to put her feet onto the stool below, the doctor detained her with a squeeze of her right arm. "Be a little cautious—both ways."

"Nobody's trying to kill me," she said as lightly as she could manage. "I just happened to be in the way."

"Which can be just as deadly."

And then, as he helped her onto the stool and to the floor, the doctor turned to Jerrod.

"You *will* see to it that she follows through with the specialist? I take it you two are very close. Am I correct?"

"Very close." Jerrod's voice was husky with emotion. "We're going to be married."

The doctor did not look up from where he was replacing instruments in a sterilizer.

"Obviously, you're getting good care—what with police guarding the door at the moment."

Police! Loralei felt a cold fear grip her heart. But Jerrod's voice was calm.

"I'll answer their questions," he said as he took her arm and carefully steered her toward the door.

"Miss Coleman," Max Avery acknowledged Loralei with a brief nod at the door. Then, turning to Jerrod, "And Jerrod Barker?"

Avery's eyes were as cold as steel, but he was businesslike as he held out a gold badge clipped to a leather case.

"I am Captain Max Avery, Federal Bureau of Investigation. You are familiar with the case we are investigating, I believe." His tone was significant. "But there are some questions we need you, Miss Coleman, to answer about today's incidents—if you are feeling up to it?"

"I—I—" Loralei floundered, wondering what Jerrod would have her do. The F.B.I. agent eyed her coldly.

It was the doctor who spoke then.

"I prefer that the patient be exposed to no more stress today. There are extenuating circumstances regarding a preexisting illness in addition to today's unfortunate accident."

"I can handle the questions, sir," Jerrod said quietly. "But I should like to escort Miss Coleman to her quarters first."

"Of course," Avery said stiffly. "Lieutenant Bolchev and I will come along, however." He motioned to the other man who stood some distance away.

The sense of unreality came back. Loralei seemed to float rather than walk toward her deck and down the hall to the suite she shared with Amy. At the door, Jerrod ignored the presence of the two officers and drew her to him, his arms encircling her slender waist bringing her head gently to the now-familiar spot so near his heart.

"Go rest, darling. And don't worry about a thing. I'll have it straightened out in no time, one way or another. Then we will make those dreams come true!"

For a moment she clung to Jerrod as if she could never let go. Maybe the embrace would have to last her for a long, long time. Maybe even forever. For, even then, deep inside her heart, Loralei knew that Jerrod would be arrested.

The two men drew Jerrod away before he could help her with the lock. When she fumbled, the door opened before she could get the key to work. And Amy reached out welcoming arms to her.

"Lory, Lory! What's happened? You look beat—and what's the swath of bandages on your shoulder?" Amy was pulling her down onto her own bed, propping a pillow beneath her head, and easing the straw sandals from her feet. With one sandal in her hand, Amy paused.

"And that was *him,* wasn't it, Lory—the Mystery Man of Mazatlan? Now," she said, seating herself beside Loralei, "draw a deep breath and tell me all!"

Chapter Twelve

*L*oralei and Amy clung together tightly in the fading light of the ship's cabin. Vaguely, Loralei was aware that the bathroom door had come ajar and was swinging back and forth in a senseless rhythm that made more sense than her and Amy's emotions right now. Each was buried in her secret thoughts—understanding the feelings of one another without the *why* of it.

Amy had listened with delight as Loralei told in part how she came to meet Jerrod. With her usual love for excitement, the story had been a "hoot" for her fun-loving friend.

But it was a shipboard romance—a starry-eyed adventure. Nothing with substance. A cruise which ended before one found her sea legs and certainly before she lost her heart! When Loralei tried to explain that she and Jerrod were not strangers, that sometimes—rarely, perhaps—love came like this when two were meant for each other, Amy's words of empathy were not there.

"You've lost your mind! What do you know of this man?"

"What does he know of *me?* That's what love is, Amy. Accepting the other person as he or she is. That's the foundation to build on."

Amy's eyes suddenly lost their look of excitement. They searched Loralei's face for some sign.

"But what of Paul, Lory? Doesn't he count?"

Paul. Why was Paul a concern of Amy's? Loralei wondered fleetingly. And how could she differentiate between her feelings for the two men?

Paul had a dream. A dream she could never share in— even measure up to. They might live in surface harmony...but was that enough? How foolish she was to have thought so. Until Jerrod!

Now she knew that a dream must be a dream for two. Jerrod and his bells. And her listening heart to his every word...every intonation of the ringing bells...

Amy broke into her private world.

"You can't throw him over like this, Lory," she said with a strange touch of sadness. "It's—it's out of character—not like you at all—more—" she inhaled deeply, "well, more like *me*—only I *wouldn't—!*"

It was Loralei's turn to feel astonished. Amy, the liberated Amy, was somehow asking her to play a minor role, put aside her own feelings, for the sake of a man! Oh, not in so many words, but the two girls were close enough for Loralei to know Amy's tone of voice even when the exact words were not there.

There was a moment of silence, broken only by the swinging back and forth of the bathroom door. And then a reaching out to one another without quite knowing why...

across the room, her dark, softly-curling hair swinging freely around her shoulders, keeping time with her rounded hips. The motions were not lost on Paul. He whistled softly, then reddened.

Quickly, he turned to where Loralei sat.

"If you will be so kind, Miss Amy Farrell, to introduce me to your friend?"

Start over, Paul had said. A new beginning. Ever the game player, Paul was.

Amy looked confused and then laughed.

"It's a joke, isn't it, Paul?" Then, without waiting for an answer, Amy went on with her usual rush of words, spoken in her appealing, whispery voice.

"Forgive us for not being ready—we were talking— but, then, it doesn't matter as we needed to know what to wear—"

She glanced at Paul's casual slacks and tweed jacket. "Not dressy! Good—and you look just right."

Amy was right. The understated sports outfit would be ideal for wearing by the "man in the know." In his short time aboard, Paul had become accustomed to life at sea and mingling with the idle rich. Already he knew his way around the ship better than she did and he had taken to the easy-living routine like the proverbial fish to water.

He loved the pampered, thought-free, *mindless* way of living. Undoubtedly, he was a part of the "in" group, concentrating more on the cabaret and game rooms than on the newsletter slipped beneath his door daily. This, Loralei remembered now, was the kind of life he was working toward. One into which he would fit—no, *dominate*—once he had captured the championship and achieved recognition...

So much to be said. Amy had no inkling of her ill⸀
or the seeming hopelessness of her love for Jerrod n⸀
Would she have confided a little of the truth? *All* of⸀
These were questions which would go unanswere⸀
because the air of intimacy, when it is easy to share one'⸀
secrets and burdens, was broken by an impatient knock
on the door.

Loralei regretted the intrusion. But Amy's face, she
noticed, lit up with anticipation.

"It must be Paul! I was supposed to tell you he's taking us ashore for dinner. This place is famous for its
shrimp—and, Lory," Amy kept talking as she backed to
the door, "there's a Fiesta Cruise that takes tourists to
the most *romantic* place—a regular gondola with singing gondoliers—that goes to the Caves of Cerro de
Creston, pirate caves, you know? What's the matter—
don't you *like* the plans? Oh, how thoughtless of me—
aren't you *able* to go?"

Loralei was saved from answering by another impatient knock.

Yes, that would be Paul. Paul needed instant response
as always.

And suddenly the room was full of him. Paul was like
that, Loralei thought dully, aware that the pain medicine
the doctor gave her no longer controlled the ache in her
shoulder. Whether by accident or design, Paul was ever
the star. Now, as always, he made a grand entrance, bow-
ing from the waist as if in acknowledgment of some
coveted medal.

"Ladies!"

Amy giggled as if there were a private joke between
them and then swept past Paul motioning him to a chair.
She herself mocked a model's slouch toward a chair

Only part of her was aware of the chatter going on around her until Paul said suddenly, "Shouldn't you be getting ready, too, Loralei?"

"I'm not going, Paul," she said, her voice sounding hollow in her own ears.

"But you *have* to! There's so much we need to talk about!"

In the presence of another, Paul?

But she could find no words. The pain was worsening and the ship was rocking. They must be getting into heavier seas. Only weren't they heading out of the storm? Earlier confusion of the day returned to cloud her thinking. Paul's voice sounded far away.

"Oh, but I had forgotten. There was the unexplained injury. Maybe you don't feel like going ashore. I'm sorry—"

Paul's voice trailed off. *He was sorry*. The unreality of all that had happened in so short a time came back. Only this scene in her mind was no longer a book. It was a soap opera! One thing was abundantly clear, however. Paul was new to the show...a new character...a character she did not like very well right now.

"You and Amy go on without me, Paul. That is, if you can get ashore tonight. Isn't the ship pitching worse again?"

Paul chose to ignore the question. His eye was on Amy whose curvy figure was turned to the closet, trying to decide which outfit to wear. Finally choosing one, Amy hurried into the shower.

When there was the sound of splashing water, Paul spoke again. Slowly. Uncertainly. As if he did not want to know the answer.

"You are all right now? I mean, the doctor said you

only needed an hour—but what else was he talking about?"

"Nothing that matters to you, Paul," Loralei said, knowing that she was right.

Something clicked in her brain then. Something she believed she had heard in the examining room: "You mean she's pregnant?"

Surely she had been imagining things. Paul couldn't have asked that...thought that of her...been so quick to jump to an ugly conclusion with their wedding just weeks ahead!

But he had. With a sick heart, Loralei remembered clearly then. And his next words led her to guess that he was still unconvinced that she was pure!

"The letter," he said in a low voice, "what was in the letter I brought from Dr. Morse, Loralei?"

Loralei bit her lip to hold back her anger. Speaking as levelly as possible, she answered coldly, "I don't know, Paul. I didn't get a chance to read it, remember?"

Let him think what he chose!

Then, mercifully, Amy was back, showered and glowing, and vibrantly beautiful in a poppy-red dress. She showed real concern at Loralei's staying aboard, a concern which Loralei waved away. But was she sure she would be all right?

Oh, quite! How glad, how *very* glad, she was that there had been no revelation of the terrible incident in the chapel! Oh, if only they would go. Leave her alone with her confused thoughts. Let her dreams come back...

And, at last, with many a hesitation, apology, and reassurance that they would be back on board early, they were gone. But not before Loralei had seen a certain look of mingled guilt and elation on both their faces.

It didn't matter. Maybe they were right for each other. But she hoped Amy had not revealed to Paul the extent of her wealth. Whatever else she found self-seeking in Paul, Loralei did not want to see him as a greedy fortune hunter.

She hoped, too, that Amy would come to see the "little boy" in the glowing body of the man—the child who needed to be cared for by a someone in the background who did not, under any circumstances, upstage him.

The ship pitched badly, intensifying the pain in her shoulder. Loralei considered another of the pain pills, then decided against it. The pills fogged her brain. And if Jerrod should call...

Dear Lord, dear Lord, let him call...

Pushing away all black thoughts, she concentrated on the day's newsletter. The storm had halted at sea, seemingly undecided which direction to go. Therefore, it was difficult to know just how long they would be in port in Mazatlan.

But there would be plenty to do aboard. And, except in cases of need or special interests, it was perhaps advisable that guests remain in their "ship home until this bloody thing makes up its mind."

Loralei read and then reread the item. Then she hurried to the elevator, pushing at the button frantically. Amy and Paul must be warned that going ashore was unsafe.

But, even though the wind was whipping at everything not nailed down, she saw that people were turning the threatening seas into an adventure, cheering, jostling, and moving down the gangplank—treating the docking more like a launching in a way which seemed to Loralei, who watched from above, like a kind of mockery.

She was grateful to see that the majority of the departing tourists turned back when ship's officers appeared to explain the gravity of the situation. But a few others pushed ahead amid the colored ribbons and confetti snakes coiling through the wind. Anything seemed possible in such an atmosphere, but Loralei could only feel apprehensive. And she was sure that the girl in the poppy-red dress and the tall, tweedy blonde man—laughing and braced against the wind—were Amy and Paul.

Trying to make herself believe that everything was all right, she turned back to the security of the lighted corridor. Surely the captain would make it mandatory that passengers remain on board if he thought there were a threat to life or safety.

Back at her cabin, Loralei heard the phone ringing before she could unlock the door.

Dear Lord, please let it be him...

And it was! Oh, praise the Lord, it was Jerrod's voice! No games. No build up. Just love and warmth that flowed from his voice to her heart over the impersonal telephone wires.

"It's all right, darling. We can be together tonight."

"Oh, Jerrod!"

"And anywhere we wish now. No more hiding. It's all in the open now."

"Oh, Jerrod—" Loralei whispered, unable to formulate other words.

His laugh was low and deep. It came to her then that this was the first time she had heard Jerrod laugh. Oh, everything was going to be all right now. The other was behind—

But Jerrod was speaking and she had missed something he said.

"—Wiser perhaps to order dinner in your room."

"No!" Her reply was automatic. "I mean, I want the world to see us together—know we belong together—that we're going to be married."

There was hesitation at the other end of the line. Had Jerrod changed his mind? Oh, no! Not that!

"What is it, Jerrod?" she whispered.

"I was thinking mainly of you and how you are feeling. And besides, we could be alone."

Somehow she knew that the last had been an afterthought.

"I'm all right. Truly, I am. But there's something wrong. I can tell—"

There was a deep intake of breath and his voice, though controlled, spoke of deep emotion.

"We can't be married, my darling—at least, not now. I'm free to come and go, but," he hesitated slightly, "I am under house arrest. But this night is ours. Oh, Loralei, do you know how much I love you?"

Chapter Thirteen

*T*he evening that followed was one that Loralei could never forget, both for its beauty and its horror.

It was strewn with the scent of jasmine that floated headily toward her from all directions as bouquet after bouquet arrived by messenger.

It was laced with soft light from an infant moon which determinedly tried to remind the storm-tossed world that its circled orb was constant as it peeked between dark clouds low in the west.

It was warmed by caresses of touch, tone of voice, and adoration of the eye that needed no words. But there were words all the same. Wonderful words—the kind that only lovers know and understand.

The first bouquet came as Loralei excitedly showered and slipped into a blue-green, floral silk dress which Jerrod said made her look like a mermaid, a beautiful marine creature, escaped for a single evening to be human with him.

And he gave her a name, telling her a beautiful fable he created about Loralei, the Beautiful, who was too sweet and pure to live upon this earth. Lovely as the story was, it hurt. It cut too close to the bone of truth—her time was indeed limited, maybe to this night.

In an odd sort of way, she wished she had asked the doctor if death could come suddenly...or if it was inevitably preceded by the periods of blindness, the pain, and finally the merciful oblivion. The nothingness...

The second bouquet came as she touched gloss to her lips and brushed cologne lightly to her ear lobes. For a magical moment, she buried her face in their wild fragrance, pretending that it was Jerrod's wedding bouquet and that a carriage waited outside to take her to the little church atop the hill.

But that fantasy hurt, too. Fantasies couldn't last. Coaches eventually turned into pumpkins. And dreams turned to dust.

Loralei drew a shuddering breath and impulsively swept her hair up and secured it on top of her head with a sprig of jasmine, letting her ears show. Jerrod would like the style. But more importantly, she wanted her ears unhampered, even by strands of hair that might cause her to miss a single word he had to say.

Then, the third and largest bouquet was delivered by Jerrod himself. And it was the sweetest of all—sweeter than the others, because its essence was distilled when his strong arms imprisoned her, crushing the tropical flowers between them, letting them drop petal by petal unnoticed to the floor below.

In Jerrod's arms her shoulder's pain was gone. Gone, too, was every misgiving in the balm of his presence. God gave them this moment. Nothing else mattered.

At last she stirred in his arms.

"Did the dinner gong sound?" she whispered against his chest.

Jerrod's voice was husky.

"I don't know," he said, drawing her to him again. It was as if, after these trying hours of flight, pretense, and uncertainty, all reserve was gone. He could not control his emotions—touch her enough, hold her close enough.

But determinedly she pushed him gently from her.

"Amy and Paul may be back at any time." She tried to say the words unemotionally.

Jerrod kissed her tenderly on one ear, then the other. Then gently he touched the shoulder of her dress to check the wound which she had bandaged with less gauze. Impulsively he bent and kissed the wound.

"Oh, Lory," he groaned, "what I've put you through!"

"Oh, Jerrod, no! I would not regret a single moment if I died this night—"

She stopped with the words, knowing that they were no longer a figure of speech.

"We've had a lifetime, you and I," she continued.

Tenderly and with ease, he took her face between his warm palms, lifting it so that her eyes looked deeply into his own.

"Yes, my darling, yes. My passport says I am 28 years old, but I never lived at all—until there was you."

Until there was you.

Four words with a lifetime of meaning. A gift from God reserved for a chosen few. And then Loralei knew with a growing certainty that her legs, her heart, and her courage were strengthening. She could—with God's help, she *would*—face whatever lay ahead...

On their way to the dining room, she and Jerrod agreed that they would try not to talk of the future anymore. Quickly, he caught her up on the encounter between himself and Max Avery.

In reality, it shed no more light on matters than there had been before. The situation was different, of course. Jerrod was in custody. One way or another, he had to return to Santa Monica where he would sign a full confession of his past misdeeds, even though they had been corrected. Then he would identify Theron Stone, testify, and do whatever they asked.

Full cooperation was in his favor, Avery had assured him—not that he had the power to make any promises, particularly until the story was verified.

Jerrod understood, he said. But Loralei did not.

"You're innocent until proven guilty. It makes no sense."

"It isn't a matter of innocent or guilty, darling. It is a matter of right or wrong—and the way I feel about it. There can be no real peace until I have righted things. Even though—God forgive me—I thought in a moment of madness of disappearing...taking you with me...trying to live in a never-never world that wouldn't have worked for either of us."

"It would have!"

Loralei realized that tears were welling up inside and they were nearing the dining room.

"It *would* have, Jerrod."

Jerrod's hand on her arm tightened.

"No, Lory. It wouldn't have. We have to get you well—"

When she would have objected, Jerrod put a gentle

finger to her lips. "We will! You must always believe that—"

Then, before he could complete the thought or she could answer, Jerrod's arm restrained her momentarily. At his tightened grip, she stopped.

"What is it?" she whispered through tight lips, seeing the muscles in his face harden. The haunted look had come back to his eyes.

Several breathless moments passed before he answered. Then he exhaled audibly.

"Probably nothing. But I could have sworn I saw our gray-haired friend lurking behind the potted palms. Avery and his partner are supposed to be acting as invisible bodyguards, but I have to be cautious anyway."

"Of what?" Her mouth was so dry it was hard to speak.

"Avery's not sure about the man—except that he undoubtedly was our assailant. He may be in with Theron, hard as it is to believe. Or he may think we are carrying the stolen money on us and be after it."

"That's ridiculous—the officers have to be exaggerating—"

But Jerrod believed them. She could tell even before he said quietly, "Don't let this frighten you, Lory. Maybe it is best that I share this instead of trying to protect you. The man may be dangerous—a hired gunman."

Cold fear gripped her heart. And for the first time she felt that she and Jerrod were prisoners. On this ship. On the sea. In life.

"Now!" Jerrod's voice was low, deep, and natural. "We are not going to speak of any of this again this evening."

Loralei tried a smile and, although she felt that it went

on a little crookedly, she felt her spirits rise again. Tonight was theirs.

The waiter appeared from nowhere, seated them with a flourish, and whisked a menu from behind him.

This, he told them proudly, was "U.S.A., Americano!" night—set ahead of schedule. The dapper, little man flashed a white-toothed smile, stopping just short of saying, Loralei was sure, "Because of the storm and the need for bolstering tourist morale."

But she and Jerrod were together, a thought which brought a mysterious smile to her lips of which she was unaware.

But Jerrod noticed it.

"Why the smile, my Mona Lisa?"

"Was I smiling?" she asked dreamily. "I was just thinking that I'm so happy being with you that it wouldn't matter—it wouldn't matter at all—if this vessel went down like the *Titanic!*"

The laugh again—low, rich, and mellow.

"Chances of our hitting an iceberg in the Southern Pacific are remote!"

And the two of them laughed as if the conversation were very, very funny. The waiter, pen poised in quick, nervous fingers, laughed too. Laughter such as theirs was contagious. As was their love.

The whole world loves a lover, she thought dreamily as she listened to Jerrod telling the Frenchman how they wanted their steaks.

"It's good to get back to down-home cooking," Loralei said as she spread butter on the first baked potato she had tasted since leaving the States. "Good to see it all—"

Her voice trailed away as her eyes took in the red-white-

and-blue streamers festooned to swing the distance of the dining room.

"Home sounds good—" she added.

Good? Was it really? When the cruise had ended... hastily, she put the thoughts in some far corner of her mind. She could forget her condition, too...only that was harder to do with objects in the room swaying crazily from side to side.

Oh, dear Lord, not now—not this quickly! Give us this night at least...

In the midst of her prayer, Loralei's eyes sought Jerrod's. His were filled with concern for her.

"Is it making you ill, darling? Would you like to go to your stateroom?"

"I'm all right," she insisted and to prove it took out a compact and went through the motions of checking her hair.

"Well, half the passengers have given up—"

Loralei snapped the compact shut.

"You mean—you mean, it's the storm that's causing the terrible rocking?"

Jerrod reached for her free hand and gave it an affectionate squeeze.

"Of course, my dear. Or did you think we had hit that iceberg?"

Her relief was so great that laughter bubbled up inside and spilled over to join Jerrod's husky chuckle.

The waiter, trying to keep his balance and maintain his dignity, cautiously approached the table again. But this time he did not join their laughter. His face was grave with concentration as he served vegetables from the silver tray.

But he tried to make his voice light.

"The steak is perfect, right? Just right for a storm at sea. More coffee, miss?"

Loralei nodded, then stirred the water in her goblet with a touch of her finger to an ice cube on top.

"Is the storm worsening?"

"Worsening? Maybe not. But it has changed direction, it seems. However," he concentrated on pouring the coffee into the now-rocking cups, "our captain's ridden out many of these and this ship's a vessel in which we take pride."

"Has the storm turned back toward us?" Jerrod's question was quietly spoken.

The sudden crazy tilt of the vessel answered the question.

"I'm afraid so, sir," the waiter said, trying to right the tray he held.

Fascinated, Loralei watched the water in her goblet slope to the side and begin to trickle onto the linen tablecloth. Then when there was a forward pitch of the ship, she reached out to hold onto the glass.

A sudden "No!" from the waiter stopped her.

"Take no chances," he cautioned. "We can replace the crystal—but not our lovely ladies. We don't want to lose her, do we, sir?"

"We aren't going to!" Jerrod said almost fiercely. The words, torn from him in anguish, were like a knife in her heart.

With an effort, she brought herself back to the matter at hand. The waiter was talking and looking her direction. He would expect an answer.

"—Be here for a later seating?" She must have appeared puzzled for the man added, "Your friends?"

Amy! Amy and Paul! They were out in this sea. Oh,

why hadn't she tried to do something—anything—to stop them?

"What is it, Lory? What's the matter, darling?" Jerrod was in the process of rising.

Loralei waved him back with a shake of her head.

"I'm all right," she all but whispered. "It's Paul and Amy—they went ashore—"

"Oh, there has to be some mistake, miss," the waiter said with an attempt of a smile. "Nobody was allowed to go except—"

She heard no more. Neither the waiter nor Jerrod knew Paul and Amy. Nothing would deter them. Danger was a challenge to them both.

When the waiter left, she told Jerrod what had happened. And she could see that he was concerned also even though he tried to console her.

They were adults, he pointed out. *Well, there was some doubt about that,* Loralei mused, but let the statement pass without comment. The waiters, marching in starched lines, were singing, "I'm a Yankee Doodle Dandy" and bringing in Baked Alaska. The lights dimmed and then went out completely so that they could flambe the desserts, and the few remaining diners would have full benefit of their iridescent glow.

It was a magic moment...a moment she must store in her heart for the colorless days ahead...and nothing must spoil it. For once, she must follow her desires as Amy and Paul were so prone to do...

Jerrod half-rose in the magical darkness, and somehow she knew to rise to meet him. His arms encircled her shoulders across the table and their lips met in a long, meaningful kiss. The kind that wordlessly says, "Forever, my love!"

Then slowly the houselights were turned up. The diners clapped. The waiters bowed. And, trying to behave as if it were perfectly normal for the floors to slant at a dizzying angle, the white-coated men threaded their way gingerly toward the tables they were serving.

That was when, without warning, the lights went out again, leaving the room in total darkness. There were the expected screams as passengers, having no idea of their destination, began a mass exodus through any door they could find in the blackness.

There were words of warning from the waiters. Words lost amid the hysterical cries of women and the angry curses from the men. There was a terrible shudder of the ship and Loralei and Jerrod were thrown away from each other and back into their chairs.

But Jerrod's strong hands reached across the table to take Loralei's. And, even surrounded by terror, Loralei felt a deep sense of peace.

Something had happened. Something disastrous without a doubt. But she was with the man she loved and she felt God's presence in the turmoil as real as if she could reach out and touch Him.

Jerrod had said it so well: *I never lived at all until there was you. And You!* she added in her heart to the Lord who also sat at their table.

The delicate tinkling of glass brought Loralei back from the spiritual realm. Jerrod's voice sounded far away in the darkness.

"We have to move, Loralei. The overhead light has shattered. And I think a porthole—"

Reluctantly, Loralei reentered the world of her surroundings. They were in danger. She should be feeling something.

"What do we do, Jerrod?" she asked tonelessly.

And then she felt it. The pleasant swish of water about her feet. Water? There should be no water in the dining room.

Think. She must think. They were in a lower level of the ship now. They must find their way from the belly of this submarine to a higher level.

Then, blessedly, Jerrod was at her side.

"We have to find the steps, Lory. There's no time to waste. The water's almost knee-high. Come on, darling, let me help you."

His arms were around her—only the arms weren't *Jerrod's* and she wasn't *Loralei*...she was back reading her novel and had, she realized, reached the most frightening chapter of all.

The real Jerrod and Loralei would be holding hands in the little alcove, the scent of wild jasmine surrounding them. But the two of them, vague strangers in the book, groped for an exit.

Jerrod was saying something about a lifeboat. But what good would that do? If Amy and Paul couldn't get out to the ship, then she and Jerrod couldn't get to shore either.

Then she realized they had reached a corridor and that some kind of dim emergency light was bobbing up and down foolishly while black-hooded figures in wet slickers went about some sort of grim task.

Somewhere the screaming continued. But here all was silent like an old black-and-white movie when the audio has gone out.

Rescue? Evacuation? *What?*

The bobbing light was green, giving the corridor a ghostly illumination. And there were people here, she realized—older couples, those who seemed to be waiting for death.

Below, on the decks, the hysterical voices rose and fell against the roar and shriek of the wind.

But above her and Jerrod there were other voices. And, with a sense of disbelief which turned into a knot that began in her throat and lodged near the heart, she realized it was the sound of merrymakers. Those who were defying the storm, willing it to continue, opting for death and insisting on one last fling. Laughing, as it were, in the very face of God...

"Oh, Jerrod!" she cried out, more in horror than in fear.

Ironically, then, the lights came back on. And all, for a moment, was quiet. Too quiet.

The ship shuddered again as if drawing a deep breath before nose-diving into the churling depths. Jerrod was pulling, half-dragging, her forward.

But she wanted to linger. To watch in detached fascination at what some television cameraman surely must be filming for the 11 o'clock news.

Chandeliers hung at unrealistic angles though. Someone should right them even though the floor was tilted crazily. Tables and chairs were skidding across the room, leaving their anchor at the upper side of the vessel and coming to squat against the lower side like scattered wooden beasts.

But things were normalizing surely. The returned lights proved that all was well, didn't they? Everything seemed quite correct except gravity. Something had gone wrong with the magnetic pole, she thought foolishly.

Jerrod was half-carrying her somewhere. Toward the deck? Where all the men were tugging at ropes? It was hard to tell whether they were letting the ropes down or reeling them in. Water was surging all around them. They were moving downward now. Down to where the gangplank usually was lowered.

Out there was the black sea. And behind them was the water it had belched up in gigantic tidal waves which apparently had inundated the ship.

Somewhere in the back of her numbed brain, she realized that Jerrod was speaking—shouting in her ear to be heard above the noise of the storm.

"Lifeboats are gone!"

Others had realized it, too.

And to Loralei's horror, she watched as some passengers had panicked and leaped overboard in an effort to reach shore.

The ship's employees, having made use of the motorized boats and perhaps all others, seemed to be working with inflatable rafts. Loralei shivered and turned away from the scenario.

How could anybody hope to escape? Anybody who tried would be drowned in the angry churn of the waters.

Or, if—and the thought was too horrible to entertain—if the ship went down, those who escaped would be sucked beneath the great hulk.

Jerrod held her shivering body close.

"Wait—just wait, darling!" His voice was all but lost in the wind.

What was there to wait for but the inevitable?

But the spiritual peace she had discovered earlier remained through the confusion surrounding her. Loralei clung to it and wondered why the rest of them couldn't see it and use it for themselves.

A zigzag of blue-white lightning dissected the black dome of sky overhead. For one moment, she saw Jerrod's face in all its beauty.

In that one revealing second, all human characteristics blended into his immortal state. And everything made sense to Loralei, even in this senseless storm.

A booming voice broke the silence between the never-ceasing sounds of the storm. Loralei listened, then recognized the voice.

The captain. The man who would have married them if one of their several impossible little dreams could have come true.

But they were frail dreams at best. And had been made without asking help from the Creator, no matter what had transpired since then. At least she had returned to His loving arms, so Loralei and Jerrod would be at peace come what may.

Jerrod was right. All was in His hands. As everything always was and would be. So what did it matter what the captain had to say?

In what might be a last gesture, Loralei deliberately reached up and pulled Jerrod's dear, dear face down to her own.

There, with their cheeks pressed together, she felt the rain dripping from his hair to mingle with her own. Their lips met in a long, gentle kiss salted with sea spray and the flow of combined tears.

Jerrod was trying to tell her something, but that didn't matter either.

She only needed this moment. Then she would do whatever he asked. So thinking, she put her whole heart and soul into the kiss. Jerrod's arms tightened and his kiss promised all she had ever dreamed of in the man she was going to marry.

Seconds distended and then contracted, keeping time with the beating of Jerrod's heart. And then time stood still. Somewhere below she heard a cheer go up. That was strange. But so was everything else. She clung to Jerrod ...heard a jumble of voices...and felt a scratchy blanket around her body. Then merciful darkness...

Chapter Fourteen

*L*oralei's eyes fluttered open. Then she coughed, rudely revived by the smelling salts somebody was holding beneath her nose.

"Jerrod!"

She tried to sit up, only to be pushed back onto the wet bench by a bedraggled-looking woman in a dripping white uniform.

"If you mean the young man—"

But her words were interrupted by the voice of a man. Familiar, but vaguely so. "Get this one to my office! There are complications with her—"

The ship's doctor. And he would want to examine her. But she must not go. She must find Jerrod...and where were Amy and Paul?

Loralei tried to protest when cold, wet hands loaded her onto the stretcher. If the men heard, they gave no indication. And suddenly she was beneath the strong, white light in the examining room. The doctor kept twisting and turning her head, mumbling all the while. And she could hear the irritating scratch of pen on paper as the nurse took notes. The only words she could make out were *stress, strain,* and *worsening.*

Wearily, she let her mind wander as, behind closed lids, little fragments of the more recent past bobbed along like the loose items she had seen on the face of the water. Somebody's slippers, she remembered. *Comfort,* the kind she would find in Jerrod's arms forever and ever. A man's hat, looking foolish because it was not doing what the designer intended: to protect somebody's head. *Protection.* That meant the loving wooden arms of a house they would build, maybe even building a high stone wall all around it—a wall so high nobody could scale it. Unless, of course, they could find support in morning glory vines, for there would be the ones she remembered in Grandmother's yard, "Heavenly Blues," and there would be hollyhocks... unless hollyhocks were poisonous to babies, bright-eyed dogs, and cuddly kittens...

But all that was past. Just a shining, beautiful dream, a rainbow-colored bubble. But bubbles were empty. And eventually they burst, leaving only a colored afterglow of things faintly remembered. Like wild jasmine and Jerrod—

"Jerrod!"

The word was torn from her lips as memory returned with merciless speed.

"The man with her," the nurse said quickly to the doctor as if Loralei were not in the room. "He left—with two men who came for him—they seemed to want to take the woman—"

"Miss Coleman?" The doctor's words were discernible

for the first time. "There's been a problem—and I do not want this patient under that much stress. We'll keep her here."

Loralei sprang into a near-upright position, causing the bright light to change colors and disappear into a red-green wheel which spun dizzily all over the ceiling. With a little moan, she sank back helplessly.

"Now, will you behave yourself!" The doctor's voice was gruff, but it carried a note of compassion. "I've other patients to care for, you know."

Shame flowed over Loralei. She had been so engrossed in her own problems that there had been no awareness of cots scattered all over the infirmary. Obediently, she allowed herself to be lifted, wrapped more tightly in the woolen blanket, and moved to a darkened corner. But she shouldn't be here. They should see that. Others were injured. And she had a job all her own.

Then again came the sense of seeing the floating objects, like the jetsam and flotsam of her life. Items washed overboard. Or cast out deliberately to lighten the vessel...or improve life's stability when there was more than the heart could hold...But what about *bodies* in those wild waves! The idea was too horrible to entertain and involuntarily another cry of anguish was torn from Loralei's lips.

But the cry was lost in sudden wild commotion. Somewhere above, there was the repeated sound of cheering screams. But here below when the door swung open it was to admit another stretcher. A stretcher so surrounded by people, all talking at once, that it had to have been brought in under special circumstances.

Somehow she knew, in the way a heart knows when the head might demand supporting evidence, that the person or persons being wheeled in were entwined in her life.

"Who is it?"

"A *celebrity*!" somebody shouted.

And then there was a din of voices, high-pitched with emotion born of hysteria instead of caring.

"But what's his *name*...oh, I want an autograph... I recognize the face...let the cameraman through!"

"Out, every one of you!"

The doctor's voice carried above that of the mob. "Can't you see the man's in need of attention? Roll the woman over here—*out,* the rest of you! This minute! I'll call security if need be—the place is crawling with cops!"

Loralei tried to sit up only to find herself bound into the scratchy blanket like a mummy. Her arms felt pinned to her sides and her legs were too wobbly to allow standing. If only her head weren't too heavy for her body—

By the time she had managed to free herself from the blanket, the doctor and nurse had cut away some of the clothing from the legs extending from the blanket on the cot opposite her. One leg, she saw, was twisted unnaturally beneath the still form. Unmistakably, the leg belonged to a man. A lithe, well-muscled man. An outdoor man, sun-tanned, and fit—

The room swam dizzily around her and Loralei was forced to reach out to a cold, impersonal corner of the examining table for support. The move brought a bark from the doctor.

"Get back! I thought I told you—"

But Loralei was paralyzed. Unable to move, except for her trembling lips.

"I can't get back, doctor," she whispered. "That man—I know him—his name is Paul Teasdale, the athlete—"

Then, supported by the hands of the nurse, Loralei filled the doctor in on the identification she knew he would need. Age twenty-five, no, twenty-six his last birthday. All-star high school and college. Working toward a gold medal—

And then the full impact of what had happened struck home. "You can't operate," she whispered. "Oh, no! Not that. It would kill him."

She felt her voice rising but was unable to stop. "He has a terrible fear of surgery—of any kind of illness or injury—and an operation will keep him from the try-out—"

The nurse led her away. And before Loralei knew what was happening, she felt the sting of a needle in her arm. Almost immediately, she was overcome by drowsiness. Then sleep.

Merrymaking stopped. Then came the grim aftermath...

★　★　★

Fighting her way back to consciousness, Loralei tried to put the pieces of the preceding night together. It would be days before she knew the whole story, but enough came back that she knew the world as she had known it had fallen apart.

Strangely enough, it was a young minister, a man she

had never seen before and would never see again, who filled her in. Her eyes read and re-read the gold lettering on the front of his Bible as he sat beside her, patting her hand and making assurances. Try to stay calm, he was saying. For the moment, they were safe. The others? Miraculously, there had been no deaths, just scores of injuries—with, perhaps, the young man sustaining the most serious.

The young man was Paul. No need to ask, for she knew the answer. But his condition? Fortunately, there were no internal injuries. He had a compound fracture, the minister said. But wasn't it a miracle that it was no more serious?

Serious? How much more serious could it be? Loralei's heart cried out. But there were no words to explain to this nice, caring man. He had no way of knowing about Paul. So, quietly, she listened as he gave her a quick, comprehensive report.

"The young man and his lady companion" both were safe, she injured less than he but in shock. Overstayed their time in Mazatlan. Storm struck. And the two of them were separated from the ship by fallen buildings and high tide. The ship, in need of repair, was at anchor—safer here than in port itself since the harbor and town had been struck full-force when the hurricane came ashore. Mazatlan was all but swept away...casualties high there...and guests were truly blessed to have lodging aboard. Inconvenient, maybe, but—

"Is he in the hospital?" Loralei's whisper interrupted the whispery voice of the minister.

"Nobody's in the hospital there, my child," he said sadly. "Winds of 150 miles per hour hit the region just before dawn, ripping off the palm-thatch roofs and destroying the sad, little tar paper houses. And shrimp boats were at sea—but about the hospital there, it's all but demolished. No running water, power, telephone service. Transportation impossible—"

"Thank you, Reverend. Thank you so much. But I have to find Paul—"

Loralei pushed back the blanket, ignoring the wave of nausea that swept over her. Above the roar in her ears, she heard the minister's voice as if it came from some faraway place.

"Paul?"

"The young man you spoke of."

Steady, she told herself. *Steady, You'll make it.* And, breathing a little prayer of thanksgiving, she was able to stand shakily.

"May I help you? No?"

The tired voice sounded helpless. He had been unable to rest, she knew, and mentally added the person whose path would never cross hers again to her prayer list.

"Oh," he spoke again, "the young man's there. In isolation. But he can have no company."

To Loralei's annoyance, the room was whirling again. Several people, all with identical faces, seemed to have joined the one who had ministered to her. She put out a hand blindly. He took it in his own, steadying her.

"And the young lady—the one who was with him?" she asked the face nearest her.

"I believe she's back in her quarters. Another passenger offered to stay with her until they located her roommate—"

Amy! Amy needed her. Maybe before Paul did. On unsteady legs, Loralei pulled herself toward the door. The kindly man let go of her hand and turned to another patient who had called his name. But his words followed her.

"Remember that the structure of life changes, but the Lord never does."

Loralei shook her head in wonder. Even in all the chaos around her, she felt the peace the young man's words were meant to impart. How wise the Lord was! He used his followers wherever and whenever there was a need. And that included her sometimes weak-kneed faith.

At the door, she turned to give the minister a little wave of appreciation. But his head was bent over a sobbing patient and she heard his voice deeply intoned in fervent prayer. She was about to turn the knob of the door, when the door to the room marked *ISOLA-TION* opened soundlessly to let the doctor emerge, a haggard man she would never have recognized except for his voice.

"Miss Coleman," he called softly. "Mr. Teasdale is awake and would like to see you. I've administered a sedative and must ask you to remain no more than two minutes."

Fatigue and vertigo forgotten, Loralie was at the isolation ward door before the doctor finished the sentence.

"I'll do as you say," she said. Then, inhaling deeply she went inside.

But no inhalation of oxygen was preparation enough for the white face laid back in total defeat against the white rumpled pillow. Paul did not look up. His glazed eyes were on the splinted leg suspended above the bed.

"Oh, Paul, I'm so sorry."

Loralei dropped to her knees beside his bed and reached for his hand.

But Paul pushed her hand away. "I'll be flying home—by emergency helicopter—so they tell me." His voice was dead. "Not that it matters—not that anything does now."

"Paul, I understand—"

"Understand!" Suddenly, there was feeling in his voice. "*You?* You understand?"

Ignoring the angry tone, she said, "I do—I understand completely—"

Paul's laugh was an ugly thing to hear. "Listen to who's talking! The fair-weather woman I was going to marry. You must have had a premonition this was going to happen!"

Loralei drew back, stunned. "Paul, how could you say a thing like that? How could you even think it?"

His tired eyes narrowed. "Then you're going to stick by, huh? Tell me that and then I'll believe you understand."

Loralei's heart died within her. And, in a small voice she didn't recognize, she heard herself whisper, "Yes, Paul."

There was no time to see his face. The doctor tapped her on the shoulder. She rose and turned to wave to Paul. But he appeared to be asleep. And there was a look of peace on his face.

Sick of heart, she allowed herself to be piloted

from the room. The nurse would accompany her to her quarters, the doctor said. She thanked him automatically.

Oh Jerrod...Jerrod, my darling, wherever you are, forgive...

Chapter Fifteen

*B*efore turning the last corner of the corridor leading to Amy's suite, Loralei asked that she be allowed to go on alone. The nurse was reluctant, but the point that her presence would make Amy anxious, an anxiety she didn't need after last night's bad experiences, won the woman over. But why was it important? she wondered. Loralei was unable to answer. She only knew that it was. Important for Amy. And for her.

At the corner, she paused. There had been no opportunity to talk last night. No opportunity even to let Amy know that she was in the infirmary when Amy and Paul were brought in. All that had happened was so unreal it would be easy to imagine—to minimize or enlarge. It would be only natural to blow things out of porportion.

She must try to put everything in the right perspective—as much as she knew anyway. How and why Amy and Paul had gone ashore, chosen to remain when there was such a storm, and the details of their rescue remained a mystery. Amy would clear it all up. She was always honest and open—

There Loralei's thinking stopped. The deceptions she was carrying around inside herself chafed in a way that was sheer physical pain. Over and over she had told herself that it was for the good of the other three that she not burden them with her problems. But the little filaments of half-truths were interlacing to form a giant web in which she, the weaver, was held captive.

Holding onto the brass rail to steady herself as the ship rose and fell with the heaving of the heavy seas, she sent up a silent prayer for forgiveness. If she could make the Lord see that she hadn't meant this to happen, maybe it would be easier to convince Amy and Paul—and, yes, Jerrod. Because now, in the reality of an ugly dawn, she realized that the commitment she had renewed with Paul was out of sympathy, not love. Would Jerrod understand?

"Oh, what's the use, Lord?" she finished. "I don't even know the circumstances of Jerrod's disappearance—or if I will see him again—*Oh, dear God, don't let that happen!*"

Inhaling deeply, she reminded herself again that she had promised Jerrod she would put it all in God's hands. They were so much larger and her problems were getting too large to hold—

Raising her head then with as much courage as she could muster, Loralei stepped around the corner. And there she stopped.

Dazedly, she raised a trembling hand to her forehead, rubbing her eyes in disbelief. It couldn't be. It was impossible. This was a chapter written in the author's bad moment, one to be discarded as not fitting into the story at all. It made no sense. Determinedly, she squeezed her eyes shut.

But when she opened her eyes, the scene was unchanged. Amy. And *Jerrod!* His back was to Loralei, but there could be no mistaking the narrow hips, the broad shoulders, and the tilt of his head. She had memorized every line. And even from a distance she could see the throb of the vein leading alongside his neck—

The thought hurt. Choking back a sob that rose to her throat, Loralei let her eyes move on to Amy. Her face was turned upward to Jerrod's. Numbly, Loralei thought the dark eyes should look shadowed, exhausted, maybe terrified. Instead, they sparkled with something that looked like a promise and the tears on the heavy lashes made her eyes look enormous. True, Amy's expression did not hold its usual invitation. But something more dangerous had taken its place. There was understanding. Helplessness. And something so akin to love that the sob in Loralei's throat became so real, she was forced to thrust a half-fist into her mouth to muffle a scream.

The plot was old. Her dearest friend. And the man she loved...she tried with all her might to tear her eyes away in an effort not to see what she knew was inevitable. But all willpower had dissipated. So, fascinated, she watched Amy tiptoe to brush Jerrod's cheek with a light kiss. Would he have taken her in his arms, said the same things to her he had said to Loralei, had Captain Avery and another man not intervened? Loralei held her breath.

"Time's up, Barker!" That was Avery's voice.

"But—but—" Loralei, stepping back out of view, heard Jerrod protest. And then all was silent.

She counted to ten and waited, breathing deeply and trying not to think. Then, composed, she walked to the cabin and knocked. "Amy," she heard herself call, "it's Loralei."

Chapter Sixteen

*H*ow could Amy seem so sincere in her near-scream of delight, her warm embrace, her laugh of joy followed by tears? She had encouraged Paul right before Loralei's eyes. And now some way, somehow, in a way that was impossible to understand, the girl had taken Jerrod.

But how could she herself feel so drained of emotion, so empty, so objective and detached? Feeling nothing at all, she allowed herself to remain in Amy's arms for what seemed like a proper time and then disengaged herself.

"Are you all right, Amy?" The voice must be hers.

"There you go—worrying about *me* after all *you've* been through! How typical of you—oh, Loralei, I've been so worried, so distraught—out of my very *mind*—and they wouldn't let me come back when I learned you were there."

The right words. The proper emphasis. And Amy's typical runon sentences. Only this time Loralei felt betrayed by what had to be false openness.

"I'm a mess." The words were anticlimactic after all they had been through, but Loralei congratulated herself that she was able to speak at all.

"Oh, Lory, I'm so thoughtless!" Amy rushed to the closet and brought out a soft, mauve robe Loralei had not seen before. Small pay for two men. Or maybe not. If they were as fickle and inconstant as Amy, it was a fair enough exchange.

Amy insisted on keeping the bathroom door open while Loralei showered. Talking simply couldn't wait. It was hard to hear above the hiss of the shower, but she caught enough of Amy's words to know that the experience in Mazatlan had been a nightmare. Collapsing buildings...natives injured by the scores... and Amy and Paul blocked away from the ship by debris, a wide stretch of ocean, and countless policia! Both of them were struck down by some flying object... and, oh, Lory, wasn't it ghastly-awful what happened to Paul?

With shaking fingers Loralei turned off the shower and began a brisk rubdown with a dry towel. The exercise absorbed a little of the fury that was suddenly rising within her. How dared this girl? How *dared* she! What did she take Loralei for, an idiot?

"Amy—"

But Amy lifted a silencing hand before any words came. The speaker, which had been out of order, was working again.

"This is your captain speaking. The good news is

that the worst of the hurricane seems to be over. The bad news is that we must remain here for a time—'' There was a crackle of static and then the reassuring voice resumed. ''—wish we could offer our guests accommodations, but damage has been severe—''

His voice faded away and then came on faintly to say something about transportation. Nobody to go ashore except authorized personnel. . .en route home. . .Mexican officials granted permission to come aboard. . .no cause for alarm. . .

The voice faded into nothingness. Loralei was about to go back to their conversation when she heard a little gasp from Amy. Glancing her direction, she saw that the other girl's face was blanched of all color. Then Amy mumbled something like, ''They've come for him—but you know that—''

There was no chance to ask Amy to repeat her statement. At the sound of a knock on the door, Amy was on her feet, wiping her face with the back of her hand, and hurrying forward as if she were expecting someone.

From behind the bathroom door, Loralei heard Amy talking with a man, but she was unable to make out the words. At last, there was a murmured, ''Thank you!'' And then Amy's excited voice, ''Oh, Loralei! Hurry—come and look—and breakfast on a tray, too— *hur-ry!*''

There was no need to rush. The scent of wild jasmine filled the suite. Jasmine. Her flower. Hers and Jerrod's. . .and yet, he had sent the bouquet to Amy. The fury died within her and the sense of detachment returned. None of this mattered. The whole cruise had been a dream—part shining and beautiful, the other part frightening and ugly. That she was a central figure no longer made any difference.

But *jasmine*. Oh, she wished Jerrod hadn't done that...

Amy had spread out the fruit, bran muffins, and black coffee and was busily arranging the great armload of flowers into a vase when Loralei stepped into the living room.

"Oh, Amy—" the words came out in a little cry in spite of herself. The blossoms were so fragrant, so filled with remembrance, so symbolic of what she and Jerrod had had—or she thought they had—such a short while ago.

Amy was glowing. "See! I told you you'd be surprised. Oh, Lory, aren't they divine? Well, for the love of Mike, aren't you going to say *something?*"

What was there to say? Loralei buried her face in the wonderful fragrance of the yellow, wax blossoms and let her mind float back for one precious moment to the impossible dream. The tears came then—tears she hated herself for, but there was no holding them back.

"Oh, Amy—" she said again, and then found she was unable to go on.

"Oh, Lory—" Amy, sobbing too, rushed out to embrace her. And this time they clung together, although it made no sense that she would be accepting sympathy and understanding from the person who was responsible for the shattering of one last, final dream.

"It will all turn out all right. You'll see," Amy

soothed. That made no sense either, but Loralei felt a sudden weariness of body and spirit.

"I'm going back home with you, but you knew that, didn't you?" Amy would rush on without waiting for a reply and it seemed too great an effort to try to stop her.

"We made arrangements—your roommate left, took the other job, you know?" Amy continued. Loralei did not know. "And I'm going to help out until the surgery's over—even furnish the money. A *loan*, mind you—so don't get any ideas it's charity—"

Paul's surgery. But she wished Amy hadn't let Paul know she had money. If he had an interest in her as a person, it was best perhaps that he not know. Then, with a sickening sensation that began in the pit of her stomach and washed up to encircle her heart, Loralei recognized her faulty thinking. What could be wrong with her, engaging in such senseless ideas when just hours ago she promised to marry Paul herself?

"Amy," Loralei began uncertainly. "Did he tell you we are going to be married?"

"Of course, and I'm happy for you—but, then, you know that."

It struck Loralei then that Amy couldn't have known. She had not seen Paul since she herself was with him. It all seemed too complicated to cope with—slanted, like the floor of the ship as it fought its anchor in order to drive back to the stormy sea and into a watery grave...

"You'll wait until surgery's over—and everything's squared away, of course, then, maybe I can make something of my life. Who knows? But you are not

to fret over what may or may not be for me. I'm not
hurt by any of this—and I hope you're not—"

Loralei gave up trying to make sense of any of the
conversation. Amy knew she was marrying Paul. And
Amy and Jerrod had entered into some kind of understanding that colored her out. She must forget about
him.

Only, dear God, I can't forget him, her heart cried.
For she knew that for her there would never be another
man. That she was still in love with Jerrod and always
would be. Nothing could erase that. There would be
no need to keep her commitment to him now, to follow
through and see the specialist the ship's doctor recom-
mended.

But she found no comfort in the thought. Somewhere
inside an insistent voice said, "But you have a commitment to God. That was the pledge you took." Oh, why
had she been so foolish?

Amy kept talking, but Loralei heard little of what
she said. The word *commitment* was floating between
her and reality. She and Jerrod had made a commitment,
a meaningless one apparently . . . but then she had made
another commitment to Paul and it, too, was without
meaning.

But she had pledged to place her problems in God's
hands. That she would live up to. *Commitment, commitment . . .* there was something else . . . oh, yes, her promise to Jerrod to see the doctor. He had given himself
over to the authorities, as they planned. Did that bind
her to follow through?

Her mind was churning like the sea. Churning with
such fury that Loralei felt as if something inside her

would burst. In despair, she buried her face in the bosom of the tropical bouquet again, inhaling its heady sweetness. And from somewhere far off it was as if she heard the silver chime of bells. But something scratched her face, reminding her that she was of the flesh as well as the spirit.

Lifting her face a trifle allowed her to see that her cheek had brushed against a small envelope, all but buried in the lush green leaves of the jasmine. A card from the sender. Of course. With limp fingers she untied it from a branch of the wild flowers and was about to hand it to Amy when she saw her own name printed on it.

"Open it, Loralei!" Amy's excited voice broke the silence.

Loralei looked at Amy with surprise. This did not fit into the conversation they had and the heartbreaking scene she had witnessed between Amy and Jerrod...

But it was as if she were not in control of her motions or emotions. Obediently, she pulled open the flap. Then she read and reread the message.

"Until we meet again, my darling. And remember—I never lived until there was you. All my love, J."

"I don't understand—I don't understand at all—"

Amy's giggle filled the room, reminding Loralei of college days. "I understand, Lory, I understand perfectly. Just know that it will all turn out for the best—like you used to say, 'It's time to be strong when hope holds its breath'!"

Another rap at the door interrupted further conversation. A messenger said that Mr. Teasdale was awake and would like to see both Loralei and Amy. Mechanically, Loralei dressed, sent Amy on ahead, and made her way to the infirmary. And mechanically, she went through the white-haze days that followed...two of them...in senseless riddle.

Chapter Seventeen

*P*aul was fretful. His self-pity was understandable to a point, but Loralei felt a growing irritation that he wallowed in it. Although he had sent for the two girls, it was plain to see that he would have turned his back had Amy not seemed to possess the knack of coaxing him to at least acknowledge their presence. Watching the two, Loralei felt like an intruder—a feeling that left her wondering anew just what Amy's relationship with Paul really was and—for that matter—what it was between herself and Paul. Somewhere out there was a man who needed her. Correction: *used* to need her...but at that point, as always, her mind hit a dead-end street and the numbness returned.

"May I bring you something, Paul?" Loralei asked the first day. The conversation had to begin somewhere.

"A new leg!" His voice was filled with anger.

"The doctors will do that, I am sure," Loralei said with more certainty than she should have, she realized later.

A wild look crossed the handsome face. "What do you mean?" Paul's eyes turned black with fear.

"*Shhh, shhh, shhh,*" Amy whispered quickly. "Lory means that doctors can do marvelous things now—and you have the two of us. We'll be with you. Right, Lory?"

When Loralei murmured words of agreement, she was certain that Paul did not hear. His eyes were fixed on Amy. And somehow she knew that the pattern was set. Paul would look to Amy for consolation. There was no pain in the thought. Just confusion.

She doubted if they noticed when she tiptoed out of the room. At the door she met a collegian-looking young man in a white coat who explained that he was replacing the regular doctor. More talkative, he answered her questions. Yes, Paul's injury was grave. No question but that the leg could be saved, but it would require surgery that only a specialist could perform. Arrangements were in progress to air-lift emergency patients...airport not open...but maybe a helicopter...

Poor Paul. Poor Amy...Jerrod...and, for that matter, poor Loralei, she thought sadly. *All of us caught in a soap-opera existence.* Overcome one crisis and another, even greater, lay ahead involving one, then all, of them. Did soap operas never end? Loralei found herself unable to remember. Maybe it depended on the ratings. And theirs would attract a large audience. *Lady MacBeth!* Fitting name for a hurricane or their stormy lives...

From the infirmary, she went to the information desk. There she learned what the speaker had garbled. The ship was indeed anchored. And, yes, there would be a two-day delay for repairs. No hotels available in storm-torn Mazatlan, but every effort would be made to see to it that guests were comfortable and entertained. Every hour would be charted...meals served in rooms due to water damage in dining rooms...and guests eventually given choice of flying home or continuing cruise.

Loralei thanked the information officer and turned to go. Then she turned back to him.

"Yes, miss?" the young man's clipped English voice inquired politely.

"There is someone I wanted—was supposed to meet—"

"Name please?" already his quick hands were shuffling through the passenger list.

"Mine—oh, his. The man's name is Jerrod Barker."

The quick fingers moved back up the alphabetical listing. "Mr. Barker checked out, miss—earlier in the day."

"Did he—Mr. Barker—say where he was going?" The words sounded awkward and Loralei hated herself for the warm flush she felt creeping over her face. She had no business checking on Jerrod. It was obvious that he had taken her more lightly than she had taken him. Well, wasn't it? Otherwise, how could he have shifted his affection to Amy so quickly? But that was her mind's reasoning. Her heart said something quite different. She loved Jerrod—loved him with all her heart. Loving meant trusting. And if he had betrayed that trust...well, she might as well accept the awful truth about herself. She had no pride where Jerrod was concerned. She would take him marked down to any price. Just how to reconcile the situation with Paul must wait.

The young man was looking at her strangely. "Did you hear, miss? I said that Mr. Barker did not say. He left in the company of two other gentlemen who checked out—by the way of the Mexican Government's patrol boat, I believe—"

But Loralei heard no more. She had to be alone. To think...unriddle what she could...and to pray.

The wild, sweet smell of jasmine filled her nostrils before Loralei was able to get the door of the suite completely open. Mechanically, she checked to see if the flowers needed water, inhaling all the while and letting herself be magically transported to the world of bright, hot sunsets, followed by the twinkle of distant stars to which there clung a downy fleece from the eerie light that mantled the Milky Way...all above a myriad of sun-kissed flowers swaying to the sound of bells...

Oh, Jerrod, Jerrod, my darling! His flowers *had* to mean something.

Reaching out then, just to be sure she had read correctly, Loralei picked up the card he had enclosed with the bouquet. Yes, it said what she remembered, and, yes, it *was* addressed to her. Nothing, nothing, could undo that. Jerrod did love her as she loved him.

She let the tears flow down her cheeks unchecked. Then, when she could cry no more, she whispered her long, long prayer—losing all count of time. When peace came, she drew the prayer to a close with a broken confession and a request for forgiveness.

"I may have committed the sin of omission, Lord, as well as the sin of commission. I have left so much unsaid, unshared—a kind of deception—even with You. So maybe I've hurt those I love the most. Paul, Amy, Jerrod, and You, Lord—most of all You. I love you all so much. Just give me another chance at life somehow—You, the Greatest Healer of all—and I will do better, Lord!"

Strengthened she rose to her feet. She had been kneeling beside Jerrod's bouquet and absently, as she knelt, had plucked a twig of the wild blossoms from a branch. Carefully, she pressed it between two pages of her New Testament. Surely it was no accident that the fragrant flowers marked a favorite passage in the Gospel of John: "Greater love hath no man than this, that a man lay down his life for his friends."

With a bubbling laugh of joy that surprised her, Loralei looked upward. "I'll go to the doctor, Lord, I'll do whatever I have to do. For You. For them. And for a possible remnant of life that may lie ahead!"

Somehow, in His mysterious way, the Lord would resolve all these conflicts. He understood that she loved Amy, Paul, and Jerrod. Loved them enough to lay down her life for them—and certainly her pride and her fears—when the time was right.

It would be easier to follow the second commandment

now—to love them as she loved herself. She owed Amy so much. Amy, her true friend who had taken her in when there was no hope for food, clothing, and shelter. Paul—yes, she loved him in the way a mother loves her child. Enough to stand by, until the trauma was over for him. After all, in a turned-around, crazy sense of the word, she was responsible for his being here.

But Jerrod! Only God knew how much she loved Jerrod in a way that was good, wholesome, sweet, and right. The way a woman loves the man she wants to spend the rest of her earthly years—no, maybe days— with. The way that made her glad she had kept herself pure. Yes, she would die for them.

"But I'll try to live for them, too, Lord—just fix things."

★   ★   ★

But the promise was hard to keep.

In the hours that followed, Loralei lost all track of time. Slowly, unwillingly, Paul's attitude began to annoy her. Wishing she didn't feel that way, she began to resent it when he seemed to try to pick fights with her, accusing her of wanting to be free, nagging her to go on, have fun, not concern herself with a helpless cripple, in the few times they were alone.

At last, in exasperation, Loralei burst out, "Oh, Paul, stop being a modern-day Job! Others have suffered, too!"

Then, at the sticken, little-boy look in his eyes, she

was sorry. *It's my own fault,* she thought wearily. *If I hadn't run away from my own problems*—

She reached and took one of his hands. But, determinedly, she squared her shoulders. It was time to set things straight as she had promised in her prayers if she expected the Lord to mend their lives.

"Did Amy tell you that *she* answered your cablegram Paul?" she said quickly before she could change her mind.

A red flush began in the hollow of Paul's throat and spread rapidly over his pale face. Turning his eyes away, he mumbled something unintelligible. But his expression was sheepish. And Loralei knew that she had struck upon the truth. Of course! It became more of a challenge once he knew the truth. And it dawned upon Loralei then that she had been blind. Blind indeed. Why, Paul knew about Jerrod. He had known all along. And competition was something to be overcome. No matter how high the stakes—even if they were other people's hearts. She was about to turn on him angrily when Amy, after a quick cup of coffee, returned to her vigil at his side. Her expression dismissed Loralei.

In the time that followed, Amy left Paul only moments at a time. There was no chance to talk things out. And, besides, Paul was in no mood. It would be like punishing a feverish child.

In an effort to push her own fears about the future away, Loralei prayed for long periods at a time, keeping Jerrod, Amy, and Paul's needs ahead of her own. The reward was a renewed serenity of the heart akin to the strength that comes to the body after a long, and debilitating illness. Now, she could pass along the strength the others sought through her without going through meaningless motions.

She packed away the few clothes she had brought, returned Amy's to the hangers carefully, and put on her very favorite, the full skirt and peasant blouse Jerrod had insisted belonged to her that wonderful day in Mazatlan. Her mind was made up now. If Amy would lend her the plane fare home, she would return to Santa Monica by air. That way, she could see the doctor again and at least listen to what he had to say.

Feeling good about the decision, she began a long, detailed letter to Jerrod. Once she knew where he was, she would mail it. In it, she poured out her entire heart—even her little doubts and fears, not overlooking the jealousies. Jerrod might as well know that she had a possessive heart where he was concerned...

And suddenly without day or night seeming to change at all, the helicopter was available, using the widest sun deck as a port. Then, Paul, wan, tired, and frightened, was loaded on. Loralei was able to do no more than—ignoring warnings—hurry forward to squeeze herself through the crowd of spectators and hold onto his hand for a moment.

"It will be all right, Paul. It *will*," she consoled, her heart going out to him in what was his greatest hour of trial.

She was barely able to make out his words above the whirring blades of the copter. But she heard enough to know that they were filled with remorse. "I've put you through a lot—" Paul, apologizing? She was seeing a different man.

"No. No, Paul, you haven't. You've just put yourself through torment—and you mustn't—"

He held her hand for a split second and later Loralei wondered if she heard him correctly. "Pray for me—"

By then Amy was back, running to his side to bring his personal effects. There were tears streaming down her cheeks as she leaned down to kiss Paul's cheek and when the white-coated attendants tried to push her aside, Amy turned on them in fury.

"How can you be so heartless—all of you—and that includes you, Lory!" Hurt and puzzled, Loralei drew back.

In the commotion that followed as the men moved the stretcher out of reach Loralei was sure Paul did not hear. But she saw on his face a look for Amy which he had never given to her. She recognized it, however. It was exactly the same way Jerrod looked at Loralei.

Loralei realized then that Amy was trying to rush past the guards and reach Paul. With the memory of Amy's scathing words still fresh in her heart, Loralei forced herself to run to Amy, take hold of her arms, and drag her away.

"Come on, darling," Loralei encouraged. "They're doing the right thing. You know that—and besides, it's time you and I reached an understanding."

In the cabin, Amy calmed down after a brisk cup of tea. With her dark hair, having lost its soft curl at the end, swept back and tied with a ribbon, Amy no longer looked like the charming vamp. She was a little girl in need of reassurance.

"Are you mad at me, Lory—have I spoiled everything?"

Loralei reassured her with a warm hug. Then, releasing her, said, "But we have to clear things between us and then set Paul straight." She hesitated before adding almost to herself, "Jerrod, too—if I ever see him again—"

"Huh?" Amy sat straight up, her eyes like ripe, black olives in their intensity. "But you're going to marry him—he *told* me!"

Loralei tried to absorb that. *Jerrod* told Amy. When? How? But before she could formulate the words, Amy, her words tumbling over one another, began to put the puzzle together. Why, Jerrod came to see Loralei, Amy said, but the officers would allow him only a minute—just long enough for her to explain that Loralei was at the infirmary. Jerrod understood...might even, she said, choose Paul for a best man when that leg was patched up. And, of course, she—Amy—would be bride's maid—maybe, who knew?—matron-of-honor ...with just a little more pushing.

Amy's eyes were shining, her misgivings having magically (and momentarily) dissolved. "Oh, Lory, we might change plans and have a double wedding— if we can just get Paul on his feet—and *you* well!" Amy stole a look at her from lowered eyes, as if she feared revealing that she knew the truth.

Loralei felt her heart lurch. "How did you know?"

"Why, Jerrod told me," she said guilelessly. "Made me promise to get you to that specialist and he'll come

join us the minute he's free—I know about that, too!
But not news, I guess. I told you I was lending the
money for your operation—''

Her operation. Amy had meant Loralei's operation?
Not Paul's! And the scene she had witnessed was no
love scene at all. It was Jerrod, wonderful Jerrod, leaving as much reassurance with her as he was able to give
until he was free. How foolish she had been not to
have trusted him without quesiton. But, then, how
foolish and wayward she had been not to trust the Lord
throughout all this. How could she have questioned
His wisdom? Jerrod hadn't. Jerrod had believed so
strongly that he had passed his strength along to her—
once he made his New Covenant with the Lord. The
Lord of Truth, he had said. Oh, it felt good to have all
this out in the open!

But her elation was short-lived. Amy's eyes were
suddenly stormy again. "Why am I so happy? I've
no cause to be. I took Jerrod's kiss to pass along to
you, but when you took Paul's heart again, it was for
keeps—and you engaged to marry Jerrod—how can
you do this to us? I've been so blind—not knowing
until this morning. Paul finally told me you had promised to marry him—and you've made him unhappy
for some reason—sending him away and—''

Loralei could hardly believe her ears. Oh, how they
had misunderstood. When truth—*The Truth*—would
have cleared away all their destructive human emotions,
their dark imaginings.

"Come here, Amy," she said gently, reaching out
her arms the way she used to do in school when Amy's
new date failed to ask to see her again. And, as then,

the other girl obeyed. "I'm going to explain everything—leave no doubt."

And she did. Not a shred of deception was left when the conversation was completed. The rest would be a "piece of cake," Amy said...the surgery...making the men understand...*everything!* If only Loralei were sure, absolutely *sure*, that it was Jerrod she loved and not Paul. Paul loved Amy, if Loralei was sure—

"Oh, Amy, I have never been so sure of anything!"

And, suddenly, the loudspeaker crackled above. The first plane would be leaving shortly...would those passengers wishing to return by air line up for inspection...lifeboats would transport them...Amy broke into the announcement to say, "Bless you for packing—Read my mind like always—so we can be first to board!"

Amy was going, too! *Oh, praise the Lord, I won't have to go through this alone!* Aloud, she said—as she stuffed last-minute things into the carry-on bag. "Oh, Amy, I'm so glad about everything now. There's still a lot to be said, but—"

Amy giggled. "Remember Miss Quackenbush we called 'The Falcon'? She used to say (Amy's voice rose to a falsetto), 'Words said make a slave of the sayer; those left unsaid, the speaker is master of!' " She paused. " 'Let all the earth keep silent...' "

Loralei took a quick look around the ship that had brought such a strange journey of sadness mixed with joy. But, best of all, it had been the setting of triumph. One day, maybe they would all return together. Then, misty-eyed, she closed the door behind her and watched their luggage loaded onto the carrier in preparation for the bumpy ride back to Santa Monica...

★ ★ ★

It all happened so quickly. A smooth landing. A vacant apartment, as Paul had said. Amy explored happily while Loralei thumbed through the mail...bills, three letters from Dr. Morse...and, yes, here it was—*a letter from Jerrod!*

The letter said very little. And yet it said everything. Things were going better than expected. The firm was hiring him a lawyer and had come up with an offer he would discuss with her after her surgery (she *was* going through with it, wasn't she? He had made her an appointment!). He would come to her as soon as he was allowed to leave the head office...and would she rather spend her honeymoon in sunny Mazatlan or in the Swiss Alps where World Wide Computers might transfer Jerrod for a time, allowing the situation to blow over somewhat but mostly giving him an opportunity to work with the Swiss on fine-tuning his idea for the computerized bells. The beautiful letter closed with one of her favorite quotations from John 14:27: "Peace I leave with you...Let not your heart be troubled, neither let it be afraid." The words of Jesus.

With a lack of fear that surprised her, Loralei reached for Dr. Morse's letters. One by one, she read them. Words. But words without meaning, because the messages, all the same, were too incredulous for her mind to absorb.

"*Come back*...new method of dealing with such

cases—risky, experimental, but given the right specialist under the right conditions... *Come back*... specialist located who is willing to take the risk... *if* he can get at the tumor in time... *if* there are no unforeseen circumstances... *if* you will consent to the possible risk of blindness... *if you will come back*... there's reason to hope for life..." *Reason?* Every reason on earth!

Wordlessly, Loralei handed the letters to Amy. She felt such a deep sense of peace that she was half-asleep when Amy let out a scream of delight, gave her a life-threatening hug, and began to chat endlessly. The four of them would live happily forever after...

Amy had found her cause, she said—and her *Cause*. She would serve her dearest friend... and, well, Amy didn't mind a bit if others chose to call being a wife to Paul "serving." He needed lots of understanding... and, in serving others, she was serving God.

Knowing she had read the message blown out to sea, Loralei drifted off to sleep...

When she awoke there were heavy bandages around her eyes. And the headache was a white-hot pain. Floating in and out of consciousness, Loralei could recall nothing between Amy's happy chatting and the pain. No doctor's consultations... entering the hospital. At each moan, there was a prick of a needle and then a friendly dark. Over and over... then a sudden clearing of her mind.

"Jerrod, I made it! *Jerrod!*"

"Tomorrow," a woman's voice soothed. "When the bandages come off."

There was a certain guardedness in the nurse's voice.

Loralei inhaled deeply. But there was no fear in her voice. "Then we'll know if I'm blind—if the experiment worked?"

The nurse was as open as she. "Then we'll know." She straightened the sheets and smoothed Loralei's pillows. "And you jolly well better be able to see! You'll miss out on viewing a lot of celebrities otherwise. Your athlete friend's going to star as an injured victor in an Olympic movie! Your Jerrod's picked up a contract—and *you* are a first for such an operation, meaning you'll hit the pages of the medical journals with some monetary fringe benefits—but why am I spoiling it for you?"

"Oh, you aren't! You aren't—tell me more—"

"No more, young lady." There was a smile in the nurse's voice. "If I tire you, there'll be trouble for us both. Now, do you hush and sleep or do I give you a sedative?"

Loralei slept.

Some of the bravado deserted her the next morning—or was it afternoon or evening? Time meant nothing behind a world of dark bandages. She was aware of a shuffle of footsteps, their number telling her that there were several people in the room. But only one spoke. The specialist, she supposed.

"Are you ready?" Loralei's lips formed a "Yes" she was unable to give voice to. Then there was an endless snip-snip of surgical scissors. And, at last, a soft-spoken command to open her eyes.

Loralei hesitated. First, she must pray. Promise God that no matter what life held she would make the most of it without complaint. She and Jerrod had *life*—and *Life* beyond life...

At that thought, his name escaped her lips automatically. "Jerrod—where is he? He knew the danger—he was to be here—"

For a moment, nobody spoke. And then a dearly-familiar hand gently took hers. *Jerrod!*

Her eyes flew open. And then, in deep despair, she closed them. She had opened her eyes to a world of complete darkness. She was blind...as they said she might be...*blind!*

Blind, yes. But she held Jerrod's hand. And she held the Lord's hand on the other side. This *must* not be the end!

"Try again," a brisk, masculine voice said. "Open slowly. The room will be dark, but we will increase the light gradually. It would have been too much—"

Slowly, Loralei allowed her eyes to open again. At first, there was only the familiar dark. Then there was a pinpoint of light...and then a halo of brightness around the face she knew and loved! Oh, it was beautiful, *beautiful*—

The doctor was right. To see Jerrod's face so quickly would have been too much. She held onto Jerrod's hand so hard that she felt her nails dig into his flesh. What was it he had said? "I never lived at all...or *saw* at all..."

"Oh, Jerrod—" she whispered. "Life was never so lovely..."

He leaned to kiss her and she felt the salt of his tears mingle with her own. "Until there was you," he finished.